THE BAD THINGS WE DID

The Bad Things We Did

Chris Archeske

For Mom,
who loves scary stories.

And for Dad,
who encouraged me to tell these.

CONTENTS

"The evil that men do lives after them;
The good is oft interred with their bones."

William Shakespeare

The Bad Things
We Did

"Hey—you're on fire!"

I look up and see one of my coworkers rushing across the break room. "Huh?"

"*Your food!*" She steps in front of me at the counter and throws open the microwave door. A cloud of smoke wafts out.

"Sorry," I say, blinking in rapid succession as if coming out of a daze.

She carefully reaches into the microwave and retrieves my lunch. The plastic container is melted, and the reheated food is so badly burned, it's black with char.

"Jesus," she says. "How long did you heat this for?"

I shrug, even though I know the food has only been in the microwave for ten seconds. I withhold this information from her, doubting she—or anyone else in the office—will believe I'm telling the truth. I hardly believe it myself.

She studies my face. "You okay? You look like shit."

I *feel* like shit. The anniversary is coming up. I never allow myself to remember it, but this year is different.

This year, the anniversary remembers me.

"I'm okay," I lie.

"Well, when you get back to your desk, you might want to look busy," she suggests. "Corporate is here, and I've heard rumblings about layoffs in our department."

I give her a knowing nod.

"No one gets fired!" she cheers in protest, punching the air and returning to her seat.

If the burnt meal doesn't ruin my appetite, her parting comment certainly seals the deal.

No one gets fired, I repeat in my mind.

No one except Dale.

Suddenly—and against my resistance—I reflect on the anniversary.

I remember the bad thing I did.

———

I WAS A NAÏVE CHILD. LIKE MOST KIDS, I BELIEVED everything I was told, and I took common expressions literally as if I shared the brain of Amelia Bedelia.

In kindergarten, a classmate and I competed on the school playground to see who could go the highest on the swings. I was winning until our teacher approached us and warned, "Careful not to go too high. You don't want to kick a hole in the sky with your feet."

When I got home that afternoon and saw my folks watching something on the news about a hole in the ozone layer, I was sure I was grounded for life.

My naïveté didn't stop there. That same year, I tried crossing the street without looking both ways to check if a car was coming. As the bottom of my sneaker touched the black-top, my dad snatched me back to the safety of the sidewalk and said, "What the heck are you doing? Are you trying to become a speed bump?"

At the time, I was confused. A speed bump? How could I become a speed bump just by crossing the road?

Then my five-year-old mind filled in the blanks of my own inquiry. I convinced myself a speed bump was the marker of some reckless kid who stupidly crossed the road without looking, and instead of moving the mutilated body after it had been struck by a vehicle, the grieving parents simply paved over their child, concealing the corpse and improvising a tombstone as a reminder—and a warning—to anyone else foolish enough to repeat their mistake.

You can imagine the look of horror on my face when my bus bounced over a dozen speed bumps pulling into school the next day. I was sure there was a massacre.

A child's mind is inherently innocent, but innocence is just a few strides away from the most vile acts capable of humankind.

I did the worst thing in my life—the worst thing any person could probably ever do—not long after my seventh birthday.

That summer, my dad was fired from his job. My parents never made a formal announcement about it, so my little brother Dale and I never got a proper explanation about what it meant to be fired. We only even knew about it because it was casually mentioned at the dinner table while I picked at my green beans and Dale played with his dinosaur-shaped chicken nuggets.

"How can they fire you?" Mom asked Dad. "After all you've done for them! After we just bought that car!"

Dad responded with a cool, unwavering countenance. He told her lots of people get fired every day. Cashiers. Factory workers. Even teachers. It's an at-will state. They don't need a reason to fire people anymore. If they don't want you, they'll just do it.

"Still," Mom countered, "they knew this would hurt you, and they should've given you a heads up."

"We've gone through worse things," Dad reassured her. "This isn't going to kill us."

If he only knew.

The following week, Dad left town for an interview in Atlanta, leaving Mom to watch Dale and me for the day. Dale was four, and even though there were only a few years between us, it usually felt like babysitting anytime we were forced to play together. I wasn't too happy about spending the afternoon with him.

Dale was a good kid, very eager and enthusiastic about most things, which usually made hanging out more of an event—for *him*, anyway. Like most little brothers, Dale tended to get more annoying the longer he stuck around.

It was sunny that day, so after lunch, Mom decided to clean the inside of the house, forcing Dale and me into the fenced-in backyard to come up with our own activities.

"Watch your brother," she reminded me, even though I knew she'd check on us from one of the back windows from time to time.

Dale was quick to play in the sandbox—or, to be more exact, one of those plastic, circular swimming pools my parents had converted into a sandbox after it cracked and refused to hold water.

I didn't care for the sandbox—not because ours was broken or counterfeited, but because sand against skin was a particularly unpleasant feeling I never valued.

I was happy to suggest playing something else.

"Let's play school!" I proposed.

My brother was excited to start Pre-Kindergarten in the fall. He had never stepped foot in a classroom before, nor had he ever attended daycare, but that seemed to fuel Dale's excitement for going to school even more. He couldn't wait to become friends with every kid he met, and he looked forward to becoming a big boy who got to do big boy things. For Dale, being a student was the ultimate rite of passage.

After my suggestion to play school, Dale promptly left the sandbox.

I figured I would like playing school, too. I imagined it'd feel good to be the teacher. Whereas most of my non-summer weekdays were spent sitting at a desk being told what to do, playing the role of the teacher would give me the opportunity to make decisions for myself—and for someone else. Who *wouldn't* want that kind of power?

Dale and I went inside the house to grab some things, much to the chagrin of my frazzled mother. She dropped her mop and yelled at us to stay outside as we ran through the house, swiping up papers, markers, a ruler, tape, and Dale's favorite *Looney Tunes* stuffed animal—a carrot-eating Bugs Bunny.

Then we navigated back outside and rearranged the patio chairs so they were all facing the same direction, giving the illusion we were in a classroom. I taped a few pieces of paper to the side of the house as a provisional chalkboard while Dale sat in one of the empty chairs with Bugs Bunny in his lap. I tapped the ruler against the metal patio table to indicate class was in session.

That's when the questions started—and my headache began.

"Why are those papers up there?" Dale asked. "When do we get to play? Why are you tapping that against the table?"

Like most four-year-olds, my brother was as inquisitive as he was forthright.

I tried my best to mirror my own teacher's behavior, smiling through Dale's queries and answering as politely—and professionally—as possible. "Those papers are the pretend chalkboard. You don't play in school; you *learn*. And when I tap my ruler, you're supposed to be quiet."

Things got even worse when I tried to take attendance. I said my brother's name—"Dale"—and watched him sit motionless in his chair without saying a word in response.

"Dale," I said more forcefully.

Again, no reply.

"Dale!" I screamed.

"What's up, Doc?" He bounced the stuffed rabbit in his lap.

"You have to say 'here' when I call your name!"

"But you said I'm 'posta be quiet!" he argued.

I never imagined playing school would be a nightmare, but it was. Whenever I said something, Dale said something back. Whenever I instructed him to do something, Dale questioned it. We went back and forth with each other as if we'd been plucked from our own backyard and dropped into Wimbledon for the match of the century. I was beginning to understand how my own teachers must've felt whenever they gave instructions that weren't instantly followed.

I knew I had to do something to end Dale's constant backtalk and incessant questioning. My brain considered the prior week's dinner conversation and concocted the first consequence I could think of.

"Dale, if you're not going to be a good student, then you're fired."

I had no idea what it meant to be fired, only that Dad had said it could happen to anyone—cashiers, factory workers, even teachers. Surely that meant students could be fired, too, *especially* by their teachers.

"I don't want to be fired," Dale said.

"Then *listen*," I demanded, and that was his last warning. He nodded his head in understanding.

I proceeded to write the letters of the alphabet on the

improvised chalkboard and told Dale we'd be learning how to read and write. I got as far as the letter F when I glanced over my shoulder and saw Dale lying on the ground with Bugs Bunny. He was rolling around and laughing.

"Dale!" I exclaimed.

"What's up, Doc?"

"You can't do that! You can't leave your chair!"

"But this is so *boring*," Dale whined.

That really struck a nerve. Boring? I was trying so hard to make school fun and educational, and I was confident I was doing a great job. And he thought this was boring? What did he *think* happened at school?

I'd had enough.

"Forget it," I said and angrily tossed my marker to the ground.

"Can we go back to the sandbox now?"

I shook my head and ripped the papers down. I told him that I was done playing with him—that he was fired from being my student and fired from being my little brother.

Dale rolled his eyes and held out his hands in front of him as if waiting to be cuffed. "Fine," he sighed and let the stuffed animal dangle from his grasp. "Take me to be fired."

I looked him up and down, staring at his round head that was too big for his tiny body, gazing at his wide, green eyes that looked at me the way a person might favor an actual authority figure. He regarded me as an all-knowing, trustworthy party that had all the answers, and he really presumed *I* knew what it meant to be fired.

I didn't want him thinking otherwise and was quick to regale the idea.

"Okay," I said. "I'll fire you."

Still clinging to Bugs Bunny, Dale followed me back into the house, once again to the annoyance of our mother, who was now vacuuming the living room and wondering what we were up to. I uttered apologies to her and told her we had to get something because we were playing school. Dale was less discreet and told her he was getting fired.

I grabbed Dale's wrist and, when Mom wasn't looking, pulled him through the kitchen and into the garage.

"I'll fire you in here," I said and quietly closed the door behind us. "Don't touch anything."

It was a single-car garage with a ranch-style raised panel door. The door was closed, but a strip of half-circle windows running along the top provided enough outside light for us to see our way around. The motor for the garage door had shorted the previous summer, so the door had to be manually opened and closed if we wanted to use it. Because money was tight and there was no allowance to get the motor fixed, our parents elected to park the car in the driveway instead. It was their cost-effective approach to avoid the nuisance of "fumbling with the damn door every day," as they so deftly put it.

Because of this blip with the inoperative door motor, the garage had inadvertently become the family's dumping zone. It was where Dad kept the riding lawnmower and red can of gasoline. It was where Mom stored boxes of Christmas decorations. It was the temporary dwelling of our unwanted toys as they transitioned from our bedrooms to the local Goodwill. It was also where various home supplies were chucked and forgotten, from gallons of old paint to stacks of extra roof shingles.

It was hardly the ideal play space for two children—but this wasn't playtime.

There was a job to be done.

"It smells funny in here," Dale said and plugged his nose.

I ignored his comment and set my eyes on the back of the garage where three stacked shelves had been drilled into the wall. On the shelves were an assortment of aerosol cans, glass jars containing various sorts of hardware, and rusted tin containers. But it was what lie behind these things that caught my interest most of all.

"Can we go back outside?" Dale requested.

"Hold on," I said. "I have to fire you, remember?"

I couldn't reach what I wanted, so I dragged a large box over, tested its weight by pushing on it, and then carefully climbed on top of it like a crude stepping stool. The box slightly buckled under my forty pounds but ultimately held solid, allowing me just enough time to swipe the matchbox sitting on the top shelf.

When I stepped down from the box, I hadn't realized my brother was standing directly behind me and accidentally bumped his shoulder. The impact knocked him off balance, and he fell back against the paint shelf. One of the cans tipped over and spilled, splashing Bugs Bunny and the front of Dale's shirt with a clear, milky substance I would later discover to be paint thinner.

"Yuck!" Dale remarked, touching his wet shirt and then immediately wiping his hands on his jeans. "What is this stuff?"

"Don't touch it," I said. "It'll dry if you leave it alone."

"Sorry, Bugs," Dale said to his stuffed friend and finished drying his fingers on his pant legs. Then he gestured to the matchbox in my hand. "What's that?"

"Matches," I said. "I can't fire you without fire."

"Oh, right," he agreed.

I pulled out a matchstick and swiped it on the striking surface of the matchbox.

Nothing happened.

Dale closely observed me as I pulled out another match and swiped it.

Again, nothing.

"Do you know what you're doing?" Dale asked.

"Of course I do," I said.

I had seen our dad light matches dozens of times, from starting up the grill to lighting the candle in the jack-o'-lantern last Halloween. I couldn't figure out why it wasn't working for me now. A seed of unease grew in the pit of my stomach as I looked at the cynical expression on Dale's face. I feared he was starting to doubt my capabilities. Dale was younger than me, sure, but for whatever reason, it was important what he thought of me. I couldn't lose his admiration. This *had* to work.

I removed a third match, this time flipping it over so the rounded match head would touch the striking surface of the matchbox. I dragged the matchstick along, carefully but with generous force, and it happened. A flame sparked. The bead of light grew as fire blossomed and danced on the tip of the matchstick.

"You did it!" Dale shouted with excitement.

"I told you I knew what I was doing," I said confidently and turned to him with the lit match. "Ready to touch it?"

Dale's enthusiastic face washed over white. "Touch...*the fire?*"

"That's how you get fired," I explained. "You gotta touch fire."

"But won't it hurt?" Dale asked.

"Remember when Dad got fired? Mom said it would hurt. But Dad said it won't kill you. You'll be fine. Now go on. Touch it."

Dale reached out an unsteady hand toward the dancing flame and retreated it just as quickly as he had extended it. "I don't want to be fired anymore."

"You can't back out," I said. "You didn't listen when we were outside. You have to be fired!"

"I'll be good this time," he promised.

"Too late," I said. "If you don't do this, I'll tell Mom you weren't listening, and you won't be allowed to play in the sandbox for the rest of the day."

Dale scrunched up his face and sighed. He chewed on his bottom lip and fidgeted with the stuffed animal's ears. It was obvious the fire worried him, but the prospective loss of his sandbox would be a huge discrepancy in his life and was at least worth some additional consideration.

Ultimately, it wasn't enough to persuade him.

"I'm scared," he said.

I groaned, my exaggerated breath nearly snuffing out the flame. I didn't expect my brother to go through with it but still found myself disappointed.

"I knew you wouldn't do it," I said.

"Wait!" Dale's eyes lit up as an idea struck him. He straightened his arms and presented his stuffed animal to me as a last-minute offering. "We can fire Bugs Bunny!"

The single flame burned brightly as it slowly devoured the length of the matchstick. I knew if I didn't do something with the match soon, the descending flame was going to scorch my pinched fingers.

"But you love Bugs," I said.

"He was rolling around with me outside," Dale rationalized. "He should be fired, too."

I cocked my head to the side, unsure.

"Come on," Dale insisted. "It'll be funny!"

I wasn't convinced a stuffed animal could be fired, but then I remembered Dad had said it could happen to anyone, *especially* to someone who wasn't wanted anymore. Maybe Dale felt the same way about Bugs Bunny after the spill had effectively ruined him.

"Okay," I finally relented. "I guess since he's *your* stuffed animal, that still counts as you being fired, too. Ready?"

"Ready!" Dale said with a smile.

It was the last word he would ever speak in this life.

I brought the lit match to the edge of the stuffed rabbit's foot. The flame licked the animal's wet fur, and a blinding light exploded in front of my eyes. Heat seared my face as a fiery explosion erupted from the tip of the matchstick. The blast of heat propelled me backward, catapulting me against the lawnmower. I coughed against the sudden intensity, my hands instinctively going up and protecting my face.

Palms to my cheeks, I traced my fingertips over the curvature of my brow bones, feeling the absence of the many hairs that once adorned it. Then I blinked away tears and looked at Dale.

I tried to scream, but no sound came out.

My little brother stood in the center of the garage, dancing in circles and shrieking, his entire body engulfed in flames. Fire and black smoke swelled upward from his burning body, charring the ceiling as he moved about the room like an uncontrollable spinning top. He knocked himself into one thing and another, leaving behind a trail of flames and hot ash in his involuntary path of destruction.

The cooked cadaver of Bugs Bunny flung from his tiny fingers.

I stood up and looked around the room, searching for something to put out the fire and save my brother. When I stepped forward, my shoe accidentally struck the red can of gasoline for the lawnmower and tipped it over. The spilled petrol pooled over the concrete and kissed the first beckoning flame on the floor, and a second fiery explosion drove me back, turning the room into an even brighter, hotter firestorm.

The little garage that was once the family's dumping zone was suddenly a raging inferno.

Dale, still fighting the flames latching to his body like hungry leeches, thrashed into the paneled garage door. He threw his whole body into it, causing the thin metal to reverberate in soft waves. Dale slapped the door with scorched palms, peeling away ribbons of his skin as it melted and clung to the metal. It was a pain he didn't feel or chose to ignore as he desperately clawed for freedom—freedom from the burning flames; freedom from the devastating smoke; freedom from my imprudent interpretation of what it meant to be fired.

Sinking to the floor with my back to the wall, I glanced up and saw the garage door activator button. I reached up to press it, remembering as my fingers grazed the button that the motor for the door no longer worked.

The door remained closed—and my brother trapped. He crumpled to the floor.

Tears fell from my bloodshot eyes, and I coughed against the thick fumes. The smoke had taken over whatever area of the garage the flames hadn't, and I could hardly breathe. Any air I managed to find came with the aroma of sulfur and charcoal.

I felt drowsy and disoriented. My vision blurred. My eyelids drooped with an unbearable heaviness.

I glanced at my brother a final time, expecting to see him lying motionless on the floor, overwhelmed in flames.

Instead, I was surprised to find him standing in the middle of the room, unfazed by the flames and wearing a strange, humanesque mask on his face. Dale's eyes stared out through two large eye holes and burned brighter than the fire. He leered at me and pointed an accusing finger.

I closed my eyes, shutting out the hallucination and the Hell around me, and my world went black.

———

I SHAKE AWAY THE INVASIVE MEMORY AND LOOK AT the black-charred lunch on the break room counter. There's no saving the food, so I toss it in the trash and turn to leave.

"Maybe bring a salad tomorrow," my coworker jokes.

I return to my cubicle, and when I sit down, I'm not surprised to see sand on top of my desk. It's appeared repeatedly over the last week, and no matter how well I wipe it clean, the sand always seems to find its way back—and in greater amounts.

Still hungry, I grab a snack from my desk drawer and take a bite. My mouth goes dry when I realize there's sand in the granola bar, too. I try to spit it out, but the sand is stuck between my teeth and trapped under my tongue, scraping my gums like tiny shards of glass.

I run to the restroom to rinse out my mouth, but when I turn on the faucet, the sink water smells funny—like paint thinner—and I decide against it.

I go home after work, and the sand follows me there, too. At first, it appears on my doormat. Then it shows up in my living room, on the runner in the hallway, and eventually in my bed.

I shake out my bedsheets over the balcony railing, and when I wake up the next morning, the sand is back, peppering my skin and scratching me all over. It's a mystery I don't want to confront, too afraid to learn the explanation behind it, too afraid to confirm my own suspicions.

Then there are the fires.

At first, the fires appear to be vague accidents, like my lunch at work. Burning something in the microwave. Leaving the oven on. Forgetting to blow out a candle. Careless shit like that.

Luckily, I'm able to put out the fires before they become unmanageable, but they steadily become more concerning. The TV sparks when I click it on. Light bulbs explode when I flip a switch. Even my phone starts to feel so hot to the touch I can't even hold it.

The fear of setting my place ablaze eventually forces me to

remove all the batteries from my apartment and turn off the electricity and gas completely.

In no time at all, my warm and inviting home is a dark and lonely prison.

Just like my brother's life after the fire.

———

THE FIRE BURNED FOR SEVERAL MINUTES WHEN OUR mother, having smelled it from inside the house, rushed into the garage and found me unconscious against the wall. After carrying me to the safety of the kitchen, she grabbed the fire extinguisher she kept under the sink for emergencies and returned to the garage. The highly pressurized carbon dioxide offered just enough respite for her to get to Dale, put out the flames plaguing his body, and remove him from the inferno. Then she carried both of us outside to the farthest curb from the house, where we were met by a screaming firetruck and its fast-moving firefighters. Apparently, a neighbor had seen the black smoke billowing out from under the garage door and had already called to report it.

It took almost half an hour for the firefighters to put out the flames. By the time the last of the flames was extinguished, my brother and I were already across town being treated at the county hospital.

My injuries were minor in comparison to Dale's. I had first- and second-degree burns to my limbs, a thermal injury to my upper airway, and a small concussion from hitting my head on the lawnmower. Overall, my recovery took about three months.

My brother wasn't so lucky.

Dale suffered second-, third-, even fourth-degree burns across most of his body. He lost both his arms, one at the elbow, the other just below the shoulder. Without any hands, he'd never build a castle in his beloved sandbox ever again.

Dale's right foot had to be amputated, and when a complication arose with an injury to his other leg just a few weeks later, part of his left foot had to be removed as well. Before he could even start kindergarten, Dale was beset with permanent damage to his body and would spend the rest of his life in and out of hospitals—and forever in a wheelchair.

The worst injury Dale bore was one I couldn't stomach—one that haunted my dreams and prevented me from ever wanting to be in the same room as him.

The fire had changed my brother's face—changed it in such a way that, for the longest time, I couldn't believe the person in front of me was not only my brother, but a living human being.

The fire had blinded Dale, and his green eyes were now lidless, milky white saucers that stared at nothing and everything all at once. His blindness was a relief in some ways as I took comfort in knowing he would never see my own expression of horror whenever I was forced to look at him.

Dale's lips had burned completely off, exposing both rows of his crooked teeth in a peculiar and permanent grin.

His hair, eyebrows, and ears were all missing, and where his nose should've been was a wide, concave patch of exposed skull that robbed him of having a normal profile. Imagine looking directly into the skull of the person you love most in the world, and you can understand how it physically pained me to look at him.

An investigation concluded the fire was accidental, and because of my age, I was never formally punished for the bad thing I did. The only punishment I procured came in the form of caring for my brother in the aftermath of the fire. Without the ability to take care of himself, Dale relied on others for survival, and my family exhausted every second, penny, and ounce of energy toward his rehabilitation—even though we all knew long-term recovery wasn't possible. Treating Dale was like dumping the sand out of the cracked swimming pool and trying to fill it with water. It was an all-consuming task with no end in sight. Still, we fed him, bathed him, homeschooled him, administered his at-home treatments, and drove him to countless appointments and surgeries—many of which never worked. We lived that life for many years.

My brother never spoke again, although doctors weren't convinced he had entirely lost the ability to speak. Dale never laughed, cried, screamed, or emitted any sort of vocal nuance to suggest he was feeling any particular way, so we never knew what he was thinking, if anything at all.

It was like he was just...*there*.

Doctors called his sudden silence "reactive mutism" and encouraged us to talk to him, even if he never spoke back. My parents did their part with this, but I could never bring myself to say anything to Dale, too afraid to be near him, too horrified to see those empty white eyes staring back at me.

And those eyes *did* stare. My parents insisted Dale was blind—"The doctors said he'll never see again!"—but whenever my brother and I shared a space together, I could feel him glaring at me from across the room. I'd glance up and always find those cloudy eyes boring into mine.

As time went on, I spent less and less time with my brother. It was just too hard for me to bear the burden of my mistake. Physically, Dale didn't change much over the years. His longstanding injuries stunted most of his growth. When he hit puberty, the doctors created prosthetic limbs designed specifically for him. They were supposed to assist in rebuilding his independence, but Dale rarely willed himself to use them.

The doctors even created a silicon mask of his face using a 3D printer, which was then sent to an artist for accurate color rendering. It was designed to be a precise representation of what my brother would've looked like had the accident never occurred. The mask wasn't terribly convincing up close, but it did alleviate some of the terrible unease I had in sharing the same space as him.

Even with the mask and prosthetics, Dale never left the house. My parents were protective of him, concerned about his susceptibility to viruses and bacteria and unwilling to expose him to something so easily avoided.

For this reason, I was never allowed to have friends over from school. This was fine with me, for I feared if anyone saw my brother and learned what I'd done to him, they'd no longer want to be friends with me. As far as the public was concerned, no one even knew I *had* a brother, and that was somehow okay with everyone.

One day, I came home from taking my driving test, my new license in tow, and found my brother sitting in the backyard, his power wheelchair parked next to the sandbox. The sandbox hadn't been touched in ten years, but my parents insisted on keeping it, hanging on to the memory of the carefree four-year-old who used to love playing in it. I was surprised to find Dale looking down at the sandbox, almost as if he were actually seeing it. I knew that wasn't possible, but somehow, my brother was conveying his innermost desire—or maybe his deepest resentment—without expressing anything at all. Then he must've sensed my presence and turned his head toward me, his wide eyes glowing behind the mask.

Sometime later, I found Dale in the front yard hiding under the shade of a tree. It looked like he was watching a school bus on the corner open its doors and unload some kids.

It occurred to me Dale was fourteen and still hadn't stepped foot inside a classroom or school bus—a dream I had taken away from him. He never got the chance to make friends with every kid he met—another wish shattered. And he was never awarded the birth-given right to be a big boy who got to do big boy things.

I had robbed my brother of *all* his passions and desires.

And instead of apologizing for it, I had completely avoided him for the last ten years.

I knew at the moment I needed to make amends, and I intended to start that journey with him the next morning.

But when Dale went to sleep that night, he never woke up.

———

I WAKE UP TO A SOUND IN MY APARTMENT.

It's just after midnight—the tenth anniversary of my brother's death, and the twentieth since the fire.

I reach for my bedside lamp, only to remember as I pull the cord I have no power.

My next instinct is to grab my phone and use the flashlight feature, but I don't have the phone near me. For the last several days, I've kept it locked away in a fireproof safe every night in fear of the device blowing up while I sleep.

The sound in my apartment repeats, this time louder and distinctly closer.

I sit up and stare at my open bedroom door, listening to the shuffling of whatever's out there making its way up the hall.

Something's in my apartment, and it's approaching my room.

Terror grips me to the bed, gluing my back to the headboard. The smell of sulfur and charcoal attacks my nose.

The shuffling sound is just outside the room as its perpetrator lumbers forward.

I hold my breath, hoping against hope the thing will turn around and leave.

It doesn't.

I look up, and it's in the doorway.

Small and low to the ground, its silhouette fills the empty space at the bottom of the entrance. Two glowing white eyes glare at me from the dark. The eyes shift in the blackness as the thing skitters into the room and disappears behind the foot of the bed.

I sit stiff with fear, willing myself to move.

The thing in the room is deathly quiet, no longer providing an indicator of its exact location. I wait for it to move, equally assured it's waiting for me.

Finally, I muster the courage to lean forward and investigate. My shaking hands press against the mattress for leverage as I slowly inch forward and peer over the foot of the bed.

I gasp when I see it.

There's a mask on the floor. It resembles a human face—eyes, nose, and mouth—and has been painted to resemble human skin, only now the paint is scuffed and dirtied.

I recognize it as the same mask buried with my brother.

"D-Dale?" my voice quivers.

There isn't a response, not even a sound to denote anyone is in the room with me.

Hesitantly, I reach down to grab the mask—but not before a prosthetic hand emerges from the darkness and grabs me. It jerks my wrist and pulls me to the floor, dragging me under the bed and bringing me to the horrible, endlessly grinning face that's haunted my memories—and my nightmares—for the last twenty years.

"What's up, Doc?" it says.

Mind the Gap

There was no question about it—the old man was dead.

"We can't leave him down there," Alvaro said from atop the subway platform. He looked at the twisted body lying motionless on the tracks below, a spot of blood showing on the man's lapel where Bret had knifed him.

Bret said nothing and wiped the drop-point blade of the knife across his jeans. The thirty-year-old was over six feet tall and weighed as much as a spectacled bear. He didn't need a weapon to be intimidating, and prior to the stabbing, he had mostly used the knife like a cattle prod. Along with his girlfriend, Carmen, who was a year younger than Bret but carried herself like the chief executive officer of their relationship, the lovebirds had herded Alvaro with that same knife out of his high-rise apartment on Baker Street, into Bret's old Pontiac, and all the way to the city's west-end subway station.

"If you don't have our money," Bret had told Alvaro, "you'll have to find someone who does."

Now *someone* was dead.

"I thought you said this guy was loaded," Carmen

remarked. She held the old man's wallet in her hands and fished through its contents, her face painted with cheap makeup and frustration.

"He's a doctor," Alvaro said. "*Was* a doctor."

"How do you know that?" Carmen asked. "Was he *your* doctor?"

Alvaro shook his head. At first, he wasn't sure where he'd seen the old man before. It wasn't until the B train made to leave the station—and the safety bulletin gave a notice to *"stand clear of the doors"*—that Alvaro remembered the old man's story from the evening news.

Dr. Winston Lancaster. That was his name.

He was a retired plastic surgeon who visited the subway station every night—not because he had somewhere to be, but because he wanted to hear the announcements over the terminal's intercom system; specifically, the voice giving those announcements.

The voice of his late wife.

The recorded tracks were somehow the only trace of his wife's voice that remained in existence, and the doctor visited the station like clockwork just to hear them.

It was a beautiful and harmless ritual that lasted several years until the city abruptly and unexpectedly removed the voice, replacing it with something current, cold, and automated.

Then the doctor felt like he'd lost his wife all over again.

Hoping to recover the recordings, he shared his grief with a local journalist, who reported the story on the six o'clock news.

The public outcry to the story was severe, and the powers that be responded to the uproar faster than anyone—including the heartsick doctor—had anticipated.

Not only was the original audio successfully salvaged, but the city removed the automated bulletins and reinstated the initial recordings indefinitely. They even gifted the doctor a personal CD of the voice for him to appreciate in the comfort of his own home.

Still, the doctor preferred visiting the subway station, committed to his original routine of hearing his wife's tender voice the way it was intended to be heard.

"Attention," the voice echoed now, her pleasant delivery in stark contrast to the horror of the doctor—her husband in life —lying dead on the tracks. *"Smoking is not permitted on these premises."*

Ignoring the bulletin, Bret lit a cigarette and clapped the lighter shut.

"Aha!" Carmen fingered a secret compartment in the wallet and fished out a black credit card minted out of anodized titanium and accented with stainless steel. "Check it out, babe."

Bret dropped the newly lit cigarette. "Is that a—"

"Black card." Carmen grinned. "The old fuck was packing after all."

Alvaro stood to the side and watched the couple regard the credit card with more reverence—more *status*—than the body on the tracks and the life it once held. Everything about the situation made him sick to his stomach, and he swallowed the smallest hint of bile rising from his core.

A sound emanated from the dark subway tunnel—the low rumble of something approaching.

"Train," Alvaro squeaked, unable to hide the alarm in his voice.

The trio had been lucky so far. It was just after ten on a Wednesday night, and other than the lonely doctor, the west-end station had been totally deserted. No one had seen the attack, even though Alvaro was sure hidden security cameras had captured the moment. And although the old man wasn't carrying cash, the discovery of his exclusive credit card seemed to satiate the demands of the voracious couple Alvaro was so hopelessly indebted to. That—for Alvaro—was luckiest of all.

But now his good fortune seemed to be running out, and as the sound of the approaching train magnified, so did Alvaro's panic. "What now?"

Carmen pocketed the credit card and dropped the wallet. She turned to Alvaro, the corners of her mouth lifting in a sly smile that left him momentarily confused. Then, all at once, Alvaro understood the gesture when he felt the sudden, brute strength of Bret's hands shoving him from behind.

Alvaro's arms pinwheeled for stability as he tumbled off the edge of the platform and hit the subway tracks with an audible crack—a sound he thought was a wooden crosstie buckling under his weight but was actually one of his ribs splintering in his side. His ensuing scream erupted as a pained wheeze.

Up top, the romantic duo turned on their heels and made for the nearest exit, the sound of Carmen's laughter trailing behind them like audible exhaust.

On the tracks, Alvaro gritted his teeth and rolled over. He choked back another scream—this time of terror—as he came face to face with the doctor's dead eyes staring back at him. They reflected two lights appearing at the opposite end of the tunnel where the C train emerged from the darkness, barreling forward like a bull shark tracking its next kill.

Alvaro fought against circumstance and through inexplicable pain. He rose to his feet and reached for the top of the platform, pulling himself up, but only just so, the sharp and stabbing pain in his ribs a newly developed hindrance to his own autonomy. He winced in defeat and slunk down the half-wall, his feet coming back to the ground between the crossties.

The lights grew brighter.

The train kept coming.

Alvaro stepped back, nearly tripping over the body of the doctor, whose vacant eyes stared up at him.

Wasn't the doctor facing the tunnel before?

The screeching roar of the approaching train brought Alvaro back to reality—back to his predicament of being seconds away from getting squashed like a pancake. He backpedaled to the barrier wall running parallel with the tracks, then ran full speed toward the platform with a springing jump. The movement was enough to send the upper half of Alvaro's body onto the landing, where he was able to hook his fingertips over the edge of a broken subway tile. Then, with the last of his strength, he pulled the rest of his body onto the platform.

Alvaro's feet had barely slipped out of the path of danger when forty tons of steel and fiberglass pulled into the station. Metal clinked and air hissed as the train docked with the platform and crawled to a stop.

Above the noise, and perhaps only because he was listening for it, Alvaro heard something crunching and popping beneath the train, and he shuddered at the mental image of the doctor's body meeting the train's wheels.

This time, he couldn't swallow the bile rising from his stomach.

The train doors—and Alvaro's throat—simultaneously opened.

"Thank you for riding with us," the voice on the intercom said. *"When departing, please mind the gap."*

———

BRET COULDN'T WAIT TO GET OUT OF THE CAR. They'd been driving along I-95 for several hours, and with no precise destination in mind, Bret wondered when and where he'd finally be able to stretch his legs.

Carmen wasn't so impetuous and demanded they keep driving.

Initially, the plan was to stop at any 24-hour drugstore they'd happen upon and make as many ATM cash withdrawals with the stolen black card as allowable. But, when neither of them could figure out the dead doctor's PIN, they had to restrategize.

"Gift cards," Carmen resolved.

Didn't need a PIN to buy those.

It was decided Bret would wait in the car with the engine running, and Carmen would go into each drugstore to make the purchase. She'd grab several high-value Visa gift cards (which she learned almost immediately had a transaction limit, usually capping at $2,000), and then she'd return to the vehicle with their new bread and butter before continuing on to the next establishment to do the same thing again.

In just over three hours, the couple had racked up a collection of gift cards amounting to $20,000.

But now Bret felt himself getting tired and sore being confined in the driver's seat, and although the rush of it all was exciting, he wondered what the endgame was and when it would come.

"We just need to cross the state line," Carmen demanded. "Twenty more miles."

Bret drove without argument. Carmen could be tyrannous, but she was logical and almost always right. For this reason, Bret listened to her, and because he listened, Carmen took care of him.

The pair only had five miles left of their journey when Carmen sat upright in her seat and swiped at her phone screen with renewed interest. "There's another one at the next exit. Phil's Drugstore."

Bret shifted in his seat. "I thought we were done."

"Last one," Carmen said with finality.

Again, Bret didn't argue.

Phil's Drugstore sat on the corner (like most drugstores did) in a small town called Plainsbowl, an aptly named place since the entirety of the town sat in a concentric circle and was as plain and unimpressive as one would imagine it to be.

Bret took the exit and steered the Pontiac into the lot. He parked the car in front of a caged locker carrying propane tanks, and Carmen exited the vehicle with her purse (and newly acquired gift cards) in tow. She could've left the cards in the car with Bret, as she didn't have any reason to distrust him, but as her mother always taught her, it was better to expect the worst of people than assume the best—even if it was the love of your life.

Carmen stepped through the building's automatic sliding doors and disappeared into the store.

While Bret waited for his girlfriend's return, he cracked the driver's window and lit a Marlboro Red.

Bret intended to take his time enjoying the cigarette—it was the last one in his pack, he noticed—but his plan was short-lived when the car radio suddenly kicked on of its own accord. Bret jumped at the high-pitched squeal emitting from the car's speakers.

"What the—?"

He hit the power knob, and the radio shut off.

Weird, he thought.

Bret took another drag of the cigarette and closed his eyes, enjoying the sensation.

The radio abruptly kicked on again, this time without the shrill frequency; instead, it produced a pleasant and familiar voice Bret vaguely recognized.

"Attention," said the womanly voice on the radio. *"Smoking is not permitted on these premises."*

Bret cocked his head. That certainly wasn't the first time he'd heard those words tonight.

A gust of wind wafted into the car, and the lit cigarette blew out of Bret's hand. The draft carried the cigarette out of the cracked window and under the cage of propane tanks sitting at the front of Bret's car.

Bret grabbed at the car door handle to go after the cigarette when the vehicle locks automatically engaged.

Then the window rolled up, all on its own.

Bret tried to manually disengage the locks and windows, but they refused his command.

What the fuck was happening?

Bret sat back and considered his options.

That was another short-lived task when his eyes zeroed in on the cage of propane tanks.

On the valves of every tank collectively turning open.

———

CARD DECLINED

The flashing words on the card reader might as well have said: *WE'RE ON TO YOU AND YOUR PUNK BOYFRIEND.*

Carmen knew it was only a matter of time before something like this happened. Either they'd already hit the limit on the black card, which seemed unlikely, or the police discovered the body of the doctor and were actively canceling anything that might have been taken from his person.

Damn. She thought they'd have more time.

"You good?"

The cashier, a poster child for Gen Z, stood behind the register and played on his phone. He was less concerned about Carmen's declined card and more vexed about how to get TikTok-famous so he could quit his dead-end job. In his mind, the faster Carmen left the store, the sooner he could work on his next video.

"Just having some trouble with my card," Carmen said.

"Bet," he replied without looking up.

Some Taylor Swift song projected from the store's speakers, and Carmen thought things couldn't get any worse.

She was about to ask the man-child in front of her if she could try the black card again when a sound—like a thousand sticks of dynamite going off at once—erupted from outside. The whole building shook, and store windows splintered with cracks as fire bloomed and obscured the view of the parking lot.

The cashier shrieked—"What the fuck?!"—and fell to his knees. He dropped his phone and covered the back of his head with his hands akin to a kindergartner in a tornado drill.

Carmen steadied herself against the counter and watched the flames outside lap at the broken windows. Then, when the fire receded from the building, Carmen shouldered her purse, ran for the sliding doors, and stepped outside.

Her whole body went rigid when she saw Bret's car.

In the parking lot, the Pontiac and cage of propane tanks brightly burned, so engulfed in flames Carmen couldn't even see into the vehicle, couldn't see Bret, couldn't make the determination if he had been able to escape the car before it—

Another small explosion boomed from the propane locker. Carmen shrieked and shrank back, hands shielding her face, her hair forcefully flying back and hooking behind her ears.

The automatic sliding doors wisped open as Carmen retreated into the store.

"Please!" she shouted to the still-hiding cashier. "Please, call the poli—"

No. The police couldn't be called. Carmen was sure they were already looking for them. The declined credit card was proof of that, wasn't it? Authorities would get the call about the explosion, hurry to the drugstore, put out the fire, and then take her and Bret's guilty asses directly to jail—if Bret was even alive.

Do not pass GO.

Do not collect $20,000.

Carmen palmed the purse hanging at her side. She stood in the sill of the open entrance doors, overwhelmed and confused in the glow of the firelight.

Overhead, the Taylor Swift song—something about lanterns and burning and a love coming back from the dead—neared its end, but the melody abruptly cut out and was replaced by an announcement, one Carmen recognized from the subway station earlier in the evening.

"Attention," the voice said. *"Please stand clear of the doors."*

Then those sliding doors clapped shut, not like automatic doors do, but with the speed and viciousness of a guillotine. The solid frame of the doors struck Carmen, held against her for a moment, then slipped back into an open position where they waited on the sides like sentry guards.

Carmen, too stunned she couldn't even scream, dropped the purse and fell on all fours. Beads of blood trickled down the sides of her face where the doors had struck and wedged against her.

Before Carmen could recover and remove herself from the threshold, the doors slid shut again, catching her at her midsection with supernatural speed and force. She choked back a surprised wheeze, feeling the pressure of the doors pummeling against her organs, pinning her like a vice and bruising parts of her body she didn't know existed.

Then the doors retreated again, only to snap back into place, faster and harder than ever before.

Again.

And again.

The metal frames of the doors bent and buckled with each impact, and when the doors struck Carmen for the tenth time, the supporting side panels clipped free of their bearings, falling aside and revealing the sharp edges of glass nesting in each casing.

Behind the counter, the cashier watched the scene unfold with shock and morbid curiosity. He blindly felt for his phone, found it on the floor, and started recording.

The sliding doors opened again, slowly this time, as if making sure both parties present were given thoughtful consideration to what was coming next.

Carmen could hardly move. Bones fractured. Insides bruised. In a bloody heap, she could only watch the broken doors prepare to close for a final time.

And they did.

The doors rushed along the track, one exposed sheet of glass catching Carmen at the back of her skull, the other right in her mouth, and as the doors came together, Carmen's head was split clean in half.

The blood-splattered doors steadily parted, staying open this time, and the store speakers continued the next song on the playlist like nothing ever happened.

The cashier timidly rose from his hiding spot. Phone in hand, he ended the recording and lowered the device. Then he impulsively shared the video with a friend, but not before he vocalized the same word he would use for the video's caption:

"Bruh."

ALVARO SAT ON THE EDGE OF HIS BED AND STARED at the wallet in his hands. The leather felt cold against his fingertips.

Cold like its owner.

Like something dead.

Alvaro leaned his head back and sighed.

None of this would have happened if he hadn't taken the couple's money.

He didn't even need it. He was bringing in enough as the mall's overnight security guard. Sure, his job wasn't the most lucrative, but it afforded life's basic necessities with enough left over for Alvaro to enjoy his nights off.

It was on one of those nights he met Bret and Carmen.

It happened at The Incline, a local dive bar that served cheap finger food and even cheaper beer. Carmen, Alvaro's server, seemed friendly enough as she took his order, speckling the conversation with a few seemingly innocent but probing questions. "Do you live around here? You married? What do you do?" to which Alvaro responded, "Yes, no, and overnight security for the mall."

When Carmen learned this, she raised a brow, went into the back room, and exchanged a few words with the brutish guy washing dishes. Then, together, the two employees joined Alvaro at his tiny table.

"Bret," the dish washer introduced himself and put his wet hand into Alvaro's. "Mind if I sit?"

Alvaro shifted uncomfortably as Bret took a seat, and after some obvious small talk, Alvaro listened to the dish washer lower his voice and deliver a risky proposition.

The couple had concocted an elaborate plan to steal from the mall and, should Alvaro agree to help—and should they successfully pull it off—promised him a cut of the profit. They'd give Alvaro a couple thousand up front, just to show they were serious about the plan, and all Alvaro had to do in return was manipulate the security cameras during his next shift, granting the couple undetectable allowance to pilfer a little from this store, a little from that one. Not enough to raise a red flag to those looking for one, but plenty to make a difference in their own lives.

Then the couple would quietly slip out, add up their haul,

and later—if everything went according to plan—meet up with Alvaro back at the dive bar and allot him an additional twenty-five percent.

Not a bad way for three nobodies to make a quick chunk of change.

It was awfully bold of them to assume a total stranger would be so agreeable to their plan.

Looking back, Alvaro couldn't recall why he took the couple's money, as he never intended to let the crooks carry out their scheme.

Perhaps that's why he did it. To teach them a lesson.

Or perhaps he was just stupid and a little power-hungry.

Whatever the reason, he pocketed the two thousand in cash and gave the couple his word.

The next evening, he watched police officers put the two in handcuffs from the comfort of the mall's CCTV room. Then, the following morning, he took a trip to a local car dealership, walking into the office with a down payment of two grand and leaving with empty pockets and a brand-new Chevy.

Alvaro could've just turned down the couple's proposition.

He could have said no.

Maybe if he had, none of this horror would have transpired. The couple wouldn't have been arrested (and summarily released with a vendetta against him). Alvaro's ribcage wouldn't feel like a xylophone that'd been played with a sledgehammer. And that pitiful old doctor would still be alive.

Alvaro opened the wallet in his hands and looked at the driver's license—at the cheery photo of the man who once owned it.

Did the old man just wink at him?

He threw the wallet across the room like it'd caught fire,

an abrupt motion that aggravated the already searing pain in his side.

His damn cracked rib. Not only did it hurt, but it was causing him to see shit that wasn't there.

He needed to go to the emergency room.

Alvaro steadily rose from the bed, grabbed his own wallet and keys, and hobbled out of his ninth-floor apartment. Clutching at his side, he made his way down the communal corridor to the single elevator at the end of the long hall. He pressed the DOWN button next to the closed elevator doors. There was a mechanical whir from the lift shaft, and Alvaro could just barely hear the elevator rising from the lobby.

He waited.

Above him, the lights flickered. Once. Twice. Then they went out completely, and Alvaro stood alone in stygian darkness.

"Shit," he said to no one.

Alvaro listened for the sound of the elevator continuing its ascent, but there was no noise within the lift shaft.

Blackout, he realized.

Everything had stopped.

He reached into his pocket for his phone, hoping to use its light to guide him back to his apartment, but his hand came up empty.

Must've left the phone in the bedroom.

Alvaro backtracked down the corridor, one hand feeling the wall as it channeled him along the dark passage. The hallway seemed to go on forever, the blackness so thick he could practically feel it against his skin.

Then he felt something else. Something he didn't think was possible.

The wall felt like cold tile.

Alvaro knew the hallway was composed of traditional

wallboard that had been painted a warm beige, and there wasn't any tilework in the entire corridor.

And yet Alvaro was confident he was touching a tiled wall. He felt the smooth surface of each rectangular tile and ran one finger along the grout holding it all together.

He kept moving, his mind still questioning what he was feeling, when he stumbled over something on the floor—a hard, solid thing lying crosswise with the passage. Then he tripped over another just like it, then another, until Alvaro understood he was standing on what appeared to be train tracks.

What the hell was going on?

Then there were lights, two of them, round and bright and yellow, at the end of the never-ending passageway. They emerged from the darkness like watchful eyes.

Alvaro froze, the lights bathing the corridor and confirming his suspicions.

He was no longer in the hall of his apartment complex.

He was standing in the tunnel of an underground subway.

The distant lights grew brighter, nearer, as the subway train pushed forward, racing along the tracks as if shot directly from a gun.

Alvaro stumbled back, away from the lights, tripping over another crosstie as he righted himself and ran.

The train pursued him—a roaring lion chasing its gazelle.

Alvaro's legs churned as he hurried away, shoes pummeling the tracks. He galloped over crossties and stretched out his arms for balance. The pain in his side magnified, and he could feel the splinter of his cracked rib stabbing inside him as his body jerked and swelled amid harried breaths.

But the pain didn't stop him. Alvaro ran and ran until something appeared in the distance—something that shouldn't have been there but became clearer and more tangible as he neared it.

The elevator.

It didn't make sense, but he didn't have time to make it make sense. The impossible elevator was the only thing that might save him from getting mowed down by an equally impossible subway train.

He had to make it inside.

Alvaro quickened his pace, arms extended, fingers reaching, feet walloping the tracks. Tears streaked his cheeks, and a hopeful smile etched across his face as the elevator drew closer and closer, its silver doors already open for him and ready to swallow him up.

He glanced back at the train, far enough back that he knew he was going to make it to safety.

With a cry of victory, Alvaro ran into the open elevator, his triumphant call becoming a screech of terror as he suddenly found himself falling, falling, falling into what should have been an enclosed elevator but was really an empty lift shaft.

Alvaro fell and fell until there was no room left to fall, and his body struck the top of the elevator carriage sitting near the bottom of the shaft. The harsh impact collapsed the elevator ceiling, and when his body slammed into the carriage floor, Alvaro's face was crushed into the back of his head.

There was a humming sound, and the lights steadily flickered on as power returned to the apartment building. Then the elevator droned to life, continuing its journey to its prior summons from the ninth floor where an elderly couple in night gowns—who had poked their heads out of their unit when the power failed—stood in the hallway, their faces wearing masks of shock and horror upon seeing their neighbor willingly leap to his death.

"Did you see that?!" the wife said to her husband. "That man just *jumped!*"

The elevator climbed to its destination, and the disbelieving couple watched it lock into position through the open shaft doors. Then, with a buoyant DING, the carriage's own metallic doors slipped open and exposed its bloody insides to the petrified pair.

Before they could scream, the elevator speaker crackled to life, and a friendly voice said, *"Thank you for riding with us. When departing, please mind the gap."*

THE PARACHUTE

They were just trying to get out of the rain.

It was Zack's idea to park their bikes at the old elementary school—a surprise to no one since most of the things they did were Zack's idea.

The school was abandoned and hadn't been used in over ten years, but that didn't matter. Its covered entrance was the perfect shelter for five middle-schoolers to ride out the storm.

They intended to wait under the metal awning just outside the locked doors, at least until the rain downgraded from a hazard to a more manageable nuisance. It wasn't until Finn—the oldest of the group at thirteen—pulled out his switchblade and started to pick the padlock that they collectively agreed it might be fun to explore inside.

"Since when do you know how to pick locks, Finny?" asked Zack.

"Since our dad put a lock on the liquor cabinet," Faith answered for him. She was Finn's little sister by a year but might as well have been his twin. If someone spoke to Finn, they knew Faith was just as likely to reply—and with significantly more attitude. "By the way, Dad's gonna start counting his beers in the fridge, too."

"I could go for a beer right now," announced Brian, pushing his glasses up the bridge of his freckled nose.

"You've never even *had* beer," Finn replied as the padlock snapped open. The heavy chains fell from the double doors with a metallic clank.

"I've had beer!" Brian retorted. "I had one with my old man last Fourth of July."

"Uh-huh," Faith scoffed, "and I won the grand prize playing McDonald's *Monopoly*."

Brian was notorious for his prevaricating. It was a compulsory habit he developed to stand out in a group he feared was more likable than him. It was also an unnecessary habit as his friends actually liked him when he wasn't trying so hard to impress or outgun them.

With the chain removed, Finn pocketed his knife and pulled on one of the doors. It slowly scraped open with a cavernous groan.

"Are we *really* going inside?" Kelsey asked, standing to the side with her arms folded. It was the first thing she'd said in the last twenty minutes, and only her third remark all afternoon. Kelsey was new to town and didn't talk much, but the group —especially Zack—liked that about her. They all silently preferred Kelsey's introversion over Brian's desperation.

"Everything's gonna be fine," Zack assured her, placing one hand on Kelsey's shoulder. She was still wet and shivering but warmed to his touch.

"What about our bikes?" She looked at his hand still resting on her shoulder and felt butterflies in her stomach.

"We'll come back out as soon as the rain dies down," he said with a smile.

Kelsey felt her braces snag her upper lip as she returned a bashful grin. She liked Zack. He had a way of speaking that always put her—and everyone else—at ease. She trusted him and didn't see a reason to doubt him now.

"Come on, losers," Faith demanded and started toward the door. "I'm freezing my ass off out here."

The five of them entered the school on what they thought was a perfectly timed clap of thunder but was actually the heavy door slamming shut behind them. They laughed with nervous reprieve and took a moment to acclimate themselves to their new surroundings.

The school was falling apart. Wires and broken ceiling tiles hung from rusted framework. Holes and graffiti decorated the cinder block walls. Leaves, mud, and other outside elements carpeted the floors. It was a dark, miserable place to be, but for the five young friends with nothing better to do, it was an exciting adventure waiting to happen.

Without proclamation, they took off in various directions to explore.

Finn and Faith dashed for the old administration office, hopeful to the possibility of finding money mistakenly left behind. They opened and closed secretarial desk drawers with feverish resolve but found nothing but old stationery, some coffee mugs, and a confiscated Pound Puppy covered in mold.

On the other side of the school, Zack took Kelsey's hand and led her to the library. He knew Kelsey was an avid reader and hoped to impress her by finding old books or magazines there. But when they entered the room, they were met with an enormous puddle of rainwater under a partially collapsed ceiling and smartly decided against going any farther.

Brian, a fifth wheel in every respect, wandered the halls aimlessly and alone. He happened upon a set of double doors almost identical to the ones at the front entrance. He pushed on them, poked his head in, and felt his face go warm with excitement when he saw what was inside.

"Guh—guys!" he called out, his prepubescent voice cracking. "Check this out!"

He entered the gymnasium—one of the few spaces in the school that hadn't been vandalized or exposed to the elements—and waited for his friends to join him with what he hoped would be matched enthusiasm. He was disappointed when a full minute passed and no one had shown up.

He shouted again. "Hurry! You *have* to see this!"

Another minute went by before he stuck his head out of the double doors and finally saw the others idly making their way toward him.

So much for matched enthusiasm, he thought.

Zack held the door for his friends while Brian ushered everyone inside. He eagerly pointed to the thing on the floor, and when the group saw what had Brian so fanatical, they groaned.

There was a play parachute on the floor—perfectly round, twenty feet in diameter, and patterned like a color wheel. Each brightly colored triangle housed its own reinforced handle, securely stitched to the edge of the polyester material for easy holding.

"Come on, guys," Brian pleaded. "Don't you remember these things?"

No one made an effort to feign interest in Brian's discovery until Zack, empathetic to Brian's feelings, offered an encouraging smile. "I remember these," he said. "I played with one in kindergarten."

Kelsey stepped forward, her face etched with confusion and intrigue. "What *is* this?"

Heads whipped in Kelsey's direction.

"You're kidding, right?" Brian couldn't believe his ears. "You never played with a parachute in school before?"

"I was homeschooled before I moved here," Kelsey replied.

Zack clapped his hands together. "That's it. We're totally playing."

"Pass," Finn said and started to walk away. "Where's the cafeteria? I bet they have old registers in there."

"Come on, Finny," Zack rebutted. "We've got nothing better to do. You can even pick the first game."

"No way!" Faith chimed in. She advanced on the parachute. "Everyone knows the youngest person picks the game."

"I thought the *best-looking* picks the game," Zack declared and brushed his fingers through his blonde curtain bangs.

"Then I'm still first to pick," Faith said. "Everyone, grab a handle."

They all joined Faith at the parachute—everyone except Finn, who shook his head in embarrassment.

Each of the kids lifted the parachute by a handle, and it made a wet sucking noise as it seemed to unglue from the floor.

"It's heavier than I remember," Brian noted.

"What's the game?" Zack asked Faith, a hint of excitement in his voice.

"Sharks and Lifeguards."

Kelsey opened her mouth to say something, but Zack spoke to her first. "Don't worry. We'll teach you how to play."

Kelsey smiled, then turned her attention to the parachute and studied it with a quizzical look on her face. The parachute appeared wet. There was a sheen to it that reflected dull light from the skylights above. She was going to ask if they should shake the parachute a few times to get the water off, but when she touched it, the wetness felt more like tacky slime and didn't come off. It was as if thousands of slugs had crawled over the parachute all at once, leaving behind a thin trail of translucent mucus that had partially dried to the material.

"Okay, assholes, pay attention," Faith began. "One person goes under the parachute to be the shark. Everyone else gets to be a lifeguard. If you're a lifeguard, you have to sit on the floor with your legs stretched out underneath. The shark moves around while the lifeguards shake the parachute, and then someone is pulled under to be the next shark."

"Who gets to be the shark first?" Kelsey asked.

"I do!" Brian blurted out.

Faith's expression soured. "But I picked the game."

"I found the parachute," Brian countered.

"It doesn't matter," Zack announced. "We don't have enough people to do it if Finny doesn't play."

All eyes went to Finn, who palmed his face. He regarded the double doors to leave, then looked back at the parachute, contemplating between the two. He didn't seem to care about the parachute—or even the other kids for that matter. Not counting Zack, who had lived next door to his family since birth, they were Faith's friends. Finn's eighth-grade cronies were out of town for the summer, and he had no one else to hang out with.

Finn looked at the pleading glare in his sister's eyes and succumbed to her beseeching. He reluctantly joined the group, picked up a handle, and turned his nose away when the acrid aroma of the parachute invaded his nostrils. "This thing fucking stinks."

"So who's the shark?" Kelsey asked again.

Before anyone could answer or deny him the opportunity, Brian released his grip from his handle and dove under the parachute.

Faith wanted to argue, but Finn gave her a look—*it's not worth it*—so she let it go.

"Here we go!" Zack exclaimed.

Still holding on to their handles, the group touched their bottoms to the floor and straightened their legs. Then they shook the parachute at chin level—high enough so they couldn't see the lump of Brian crawling underneath the parachute but low enough so none of them could sneak a peek and determine who he was targeting.

The game had begun.

They sat for half a minute shaking the parachute, waiting with bated breath for Brian to make his move.

Finn looked to Zack, and Zack looked to Kelsey, who was wondering if this was how long the game usually took.

"Is he going to pick somebody?" Kelsey asked over the flapping sound of the parachute.

No one understood what was taking so long for Brian to choose his victim.

Faith impatiently rolled her eyes. "Jesus, Brian, just pick—"

Her words faltered as she was suddenly and violently yanked under the parachute. Faith's back hit the floor with a heavy slap, and her head drummed against the wood in a series of rapid, painful blows as she was partially dragged under.

Kelsey gasped in surprise and dropped her handle.

Everyone stopped the game and watched Faith surface from one side of the parachute and Brian the other.

"What happened?" Brian asked, fixing the glasses on his face. He looked at his friends and wondered why they were staring at him with an accusing eye.

Faith rubbed the back of her pained head. "Brian, that hurt!"

"What are you talking about?" he asked.

"Why did you pull me like that?"

"Huh? I didn't pull you."

"Yes, you did! You grabbed my shoe!"

"I swear, I didn't!"

"Maybe we should play a new game," Kelsey suggested, feeling uncomfortable.

"Seriously, dude, why did you grab her so hard?" Zack asked Brian.

"I'm telling you—I didn't touch her!" Brian maintained. "I didn't touch *anyone!*"

"This is better than I thought it was going to be," Finn added and flinched when Faith slugged him on the arm.

"Kelsey's right," Zack proclaimed. "Let's just play another game."

"Maybe one where we don't fucking touch each other," Faith proposed, still coddling the back of her head. "I didn't realize that was going to be such a problem."

"I didn't touch you!" Brian asserted. Now he was irritated. Hadn't they noticed he was fixing his glasses under the parachute when Faith was pulled? He recalled diving under the parachute and feeling his glasses slip from his face the moment he was on all fours. He was so busy searching for them, he spent his entire turn mirroring Velma from *Scooby-Doo* and didn't actually get a chance to be the shark.

"Let's play Don't Get Caught," suggested Zack, playing arbitrator. "That game's zero contact. The only thing that might touch us is the parachute."

Brian sighed and returned to his handle. He realized his friends had made up their minds about what happened, and there was no use in trying to convince them otherwise.

"How do we play?" inquired Kelsey.

"Everyone raises the parachute as high as possible," Zack explained, "and then we take turns running under it from one side to the other before the parachute falls on us. If the parachute touches you, you're out."

"Brian can go last," Faith suggested.

"I didn't do anything!" Brian snapped. He nearly let go of the parachute and stormed off, but Zack reached out a calming hand and got him to stay.

"I'll call out a name first," Zack said, "and whoever I choose can call the next person—and so on. Any questions?"

"Don't call me first," Kelsey pleaded.

"Don't call me at all," remarked Finn. He was ready to be done with this baby shit and move on to something else.

With no other pronouncements, the group started the game. Together, they lifted the parachute high above their heads, with Kelsey and Faith unconsciously standing on tiptoes to match the height of the boys. The parachute sailed upward in the shape of a mushroom cloud.

Zack called out the first name. "Finny!"

Finn shot Zack a look—*you're an ass*. Then he released his grip from the handle and ran under the plunging parachute.

Finn was halfway across when, to the group's surprise, he abruptly froze. He stood motionless under the center of the parachute as if someone had pressed a real-life pause button.

"Um, Finn, what are you doing?" Faith inquired.

Her brother didn't move or say anything. He didn't even blink. No one knew what was happening or what was wrong, but it became obvious from the sheer look of horror on Finn's face something wasn't right.

"Finny...?" Zack breathed.

Finn stared into empty space, eyes bulging, his brow curving downward in an expression of pure terror.

Zack glanced at Kelsey, who observed the scene with a knot in her stomach.

The only movement came from the parachute continuing its descent, closing the gap between itself and the top of Finn's head—but Finn still didn't move.

Just when Kelsey was sure something horrible was going to happen, Finn grinned—a wide, intentional grin that might as well have been Finn screaming, *"Gotcha, assholes!"*

Then Finn started doing the Cabbage Patch.

Everyone but Kelsey laughed at Finn's sudden dance break.

Finn raced forward, cleared the path of the parachute, and

emerged from the other side just in the nick of time. As the parachute touched the floor, Finn bowed.

"You're an idiot!" Faith bellowed. "Stupidity better not run in the family!"

Finn shot her the bird.

Kelsey wanted to tell Finn he wasn't funny—that he really scared her and made her believe something was wrong. At the same time, Kelsey knew she was tightly wound after what happened to Faith, and she didn't want to appear weak or overly sensitive to her newfound friends. She bit her tongue.

"Your turn to call someone, Finny!" Zack prompted.

The parachute went up again.

"Faith!" Finn called.

The game continued with Faith choosing Zack, and Zack choosing Kelsey.

Kelsey was able to clear the twenty-foot distance without being touched by the parachute, but something in her gut told her she shouldn't be playing with the parachute—that *none* of them should be playing with it. But for what reason? They were all having a good time with it—right?

Even Faith seemed more forgiving—or at least more forgetful—of her accusation against Brian and was enjoying herself.

So why did Kelsey feel so uneasy?

Maybe nothing even happened to Faith, Kelsey thought. Maybe she dragged *herself* under the parachute, the same way Finn pretended something was wrong with him just moments ago. Kelsey learned early on they all liked pranking each other from time to time.

She convinced herself she was being ridiculous. It was just a parachute.

"Kelsey, your turn to pick," Zack reminded her.

Kelsey trained her eyes on the only person who hadn't had a turn and called his name: "Brian!"

The parachute went up, and twelve-year-old Brian went under.

Brian had only taken a few steps when his sneaker found a splash of rainwater on the floor, probably left behind by the others running back and forth before him. He slipped and fell forward, the wind escaping his lungs as the maple floor slammed into his chest. His glasses flew from his face. His jaw recoiled against the hardwood, chattering his teeth. It was as painful as it was graceless.

Brian rolled over onto his back, expecting to hear cries of worry from his friends, maybe even a nervous laugh or two, but when he looked around, he could see everyone but Kelsey rolling their eyes.

"Way to go, clutzo," Faith groaned.

They weren't worried. They were just annoyed with him.

Brian dropped his head back, defeated, and took a moment to catch his breath. He looked up at the dome-shaped parachute steadily descending on him and curiously cocked his head to the side when he saw it.

There was something attached to the underside of the parachute.

He wasn't wearing his glasses for the clearest image, but Brian could see it well enough to distinguish it was thin, transparent, and had spread across the entire undersurface of the parachute, much like the sticky film Kelsey had seen on top.

But this thing was different from the slime. It had formed to the parachute the way a fruitcake molds to its baking tin. It was gelatinous, maybe half a centimeter thick, and plaited with fibrous purple veins like a membranous sac. From his angle, it's what Brian imagined peering into the subumbrella of a giant jellyfish might look like.

The thing rippled in soft waves, somehow independent of the parachute but attached to its underside like an unwanted parasite.

Whatever the thing was, it was moving.

It was moving because it was alive.

This is why the parachute felt so heavy, Brian realized. *This is what grabbed Faith.*

The parachute floated downward, bringing the organism with it. Now Brian could see its braided veins in better detail, pumping blood—he guessed it was blood—across a spiderweb of vessels that made up the thing's vascular system, assuming it had one.

Brian's mouth hung open in awe and disbelief, too stunned to alert the others to what he was seeing, too enamored by its presence to realize the path for him to escape had narrowed from grim to impossible.

His fate was sealed.

The parachute—and the entity underneath it—fell over Brian.

The thing touched his skin, and he screamed.

It burned.

It burned because it instantly seared Brian's flesh and disintegrated his skin like some kind of superacid. Brian kicked and bucked and thrashed around to rid himself of the monstrosity, but it had already stuck to him, holding as tightly to him as it did the parachute.

"HELP ME HELP ME IT BURNS HELP MEEEEUGGHH—"

The group watched Brian flail and scream under the parachute like a toddler not wanting to get out of bed in the morning, but no one made an effort to help or even offer a reaction of concern. For them, this was just another one of Brian's attention-seeking acts of desperation, and they didn't want to play any part in entertaining it and seeing it repeated later.

"You can stop, Brian," Faith mumbled. "It wasn't funny when Finn did it."

"I didn't do *that*," Finn said.

"Brian, just come out," Zack insisted.

Under the parachute, Brian's muffled cries became foamy gurgles as his freckled nose dissolved into a pool of blood. His pink lips burned away, and the entirety of his face melted into the thing, floating into its viscid form before running away in fine, crimson rivers.

The thing wasn't just putrefying Brian.

It was *absorbing* him.

Unable to breathe, Brian desperately scratched at the thing. It disintegrated his fingers down to the knuckles, then his knuckles to the wrists, and his wrists to the elbows. The thing lapped up every morsel of him. The more of his body it absorbed, the faster it ate him.

Brian's pain reached a crescendo—an agony so unbearable and excruciating that for the briefest of moments he didn't feel anything at all. Then the thing melted his frontal bone and touched his brain, and Brian's body—or what was left of it— went still.

The group looked on at the motionless lump at the center of the parachute. They couldn't see Brian, but they still expected the boy-shaped bump to sit up, turn over, or start crawling to the edge. When none of these things happened, and the lump that was Brian still hadn't moved or said anything, they looked at each other with similarly confused expressions.

"Brian?" Zack spoke, and Kelsey noticed the slightest hint of worry in his voice. It was somehow comforting because she was starting to worry, too.

"Quit fucking around, Brian!" Faith scolded, less concerned and more aggravated.

"I'm over this," Finn said and glanced up at the skylights. "The rain stopped. I'm getting out of here." He dropped his handle and made for the double doors to leave. Faith was quick to follow.

Kelsey glanced at Zack, unsure if she should stay with him or follow the others out.

"Guys, wait!" Zack demanded and pointed to the parachute. "Something—something's happening."

He was right. Something *was* happening.

The lump at the center of the parachute was moving again.

No. Not moving.

Sinking.

To their untrained eyes, it looked like Brian was being sucked into the floor.

When Finn and Faith saw this from the doors, they questioned what they were seeing and curiously returned to the parachute for a closer look.

"How is he doing that?" Faith asked.

"Something's wrong," Kelsey said.

"Quick, help me lift this!" Zack gestured to the parachute with a small flick of his handle.

Finn and Faith obliged their friend and grabbed their handles.

The four of them looked at each other and nodded in agreement. Then they collectively snapped the parachute into the air the way their mothers might flick a clean shirt fresh out of the dryer.

The parachute wafted toward the ceiling.

As the parachute billowed upward, the melted lump that was Brian went with it. His half-eaten carcass hovered above the group like a ghoulish balloon animal in a Thanksgiving Day parade—but Brian's sticky body didn't stay bonded to the parachute for long. As the parachute reached its peak, his gooey remains steadily separated from it. He slowly floated downward from a collection of sinewy strings that resembled hot cheese on a slice of pizza being pulled away from the pie.

Kelsey was the first to gasp, and the only one to drop her handle in time.

The thing under the domed parachute suddenly slithered down and covered every nylon handle, including the ones held by Faith, Finn, and Zack.

"Ow, what the fuck—" Finn managed to say before the translucent blob on his hand turned pink with his blood.

"What the hell is this ouch OH MY GOD GET IT OFF ME!" Faith cried, and she shrieked as the thing rapidly molted her fingers.

Zack, too stunned to speak, too horrified to react, silently watched the thing slip across his hands and gradually pool over his wrists. It wasn't until he saw his skin bubble underneath that he finally let out a blood-curdling scream of terror.

"OH GOD GET IT OFF OH GODDDDDDD—"

Each of them tried letting go of their handles, but the thing had them at its mercy. It melted their palms and fused them to the parachute, preventing their escape.

Then it started eating them, beginning with their fingertips and working quickly up their arms.

Their screams were otherworldly, a response to a pain so dreadful it defied the bounds of human understanding.

Kelsey, her pale face stricken with tears, glanced at Zack—the boy who held the door for her; the boy who made sure she was always comfortable in a group full of strangers; the boy who gave her butterflies when he smiled at her; and now the boy melting in front of her eyes and screaming for her to save him.

"KELSEY HELP ME OH GOD PLEASE HELP MEEEE KELSEY HELP MEEEEE—"

Kelsey stood rooted to the spot, listening to Zack's cries for help—to *all* their cries.

Then the tortured three collapsed to their knees, just as the parachute finally descended on them. It fell over their bodies like a fire blanket, extinguishing the horror and ending their screams of agony.

Kelsey ran. She exploded out of the gym's double doors, her breaths coming quickly and in panicked succession. She imagined the parachute drifting across the floor and rushing the empty corridors to catch her, convinced she could hear it whooshing and rustling not far behind. But she didn't look back, not even for a cursory glance, too afraid the parachute would suddenly fall over her and swallow her up like a fast-moving tidal wave.

Kelsey ran and ran until she came to the exit doors and escaped to the safety of the schoolyard. She felt the warm kiss of sunlight on her skin, smelled the pleasant aroma of the wet grass, and heard the gentle singsong of the birds in the trees. The sudden calm was unnerving, and the incredulity that this was what the outside world looked like while her friends were dying in the shadows was enough to overwhelm Kelsey and bring her to her knees.

She finally screamed.

WHEN THE POLICE ARRIVED AT THE OLD SCHOOL with Kelsey and her parents sometime later, the parachute—and the thing underneath it—were already gone. No bodies were discovered, a nonsurprise to Kelsey, who was certain the thing had entirely consumed them by then.

Kelsey imagined the thing feeling full from its meal, moving on to its next hunting ground, toting the parachute along like a hermit crab carrying its shell. But how far could a colorful, twenty-foot parachute go without being seen?

No one believed Kelsey about what happened to her friends, and over the next few months, Kelsey withdrew from the world—even more than usual. She didn't socialize. She barely ate. She removed herself from the public eye and went back to being homeschooled. She only went outside to go to her therapy appointments—a task more difficult than expected when she saw the faces of her former friends staring back at her from the various missing persons posters plastered across town.

When she went to sleep at night, Kelsey dreamed of those same faces leering at her from the darkness. She dreamed of Zack standing in the corner of her bedroom, pointing at her with his bloody stumps, his wide eyes burning like hot coals as he pleaded to her in a nightmarish, guttural whisper from beyond the grave.

"Kelseyyyy...help meeee...it hurtsssss...don't leave meeee..."

Then Zack's face would melt away into a pit of gore, and Kelsey would bolt awake in a night sweat so severe, the perspiration had soaked through her clothes, her bedsheets, and even the mattress protector her mom thought would help.

Perhaps the most unexpected trauma, and even worse than not being believed about the parachute, were the rumors Kelsey had played an active role in the quartet's disappearance—that she more than likely killed her friends and hid their bodies herself. Eventually, the rumors became so mainstream that Kelsey feared her parents, the police, and even her therapist believed she played a part.

Kelsey had survived the parachute, but the painful reminders, bad dreams, and awful accusations against her sometimes made her wish she had never let go of it.

———

WHEN KELSEY TURNED EIGHTEEN, SHE LEFT TOWN and never looked back. She moved five states over, putting a thousand miles between herself and her past, determined to escape a life that haunted her.

She went to college and got a job at a public library stocking shelves. Within a year, she was promoted to front desk library assistant and, after graduating, became the new media specialist at the town's high school.

One day, while attending a required district workshop, Kelsey would meet another librarian named Tom—a kind and handsome man who would ultimately become her confidant, her husband, and the father of her three children.

Together, they would buy a house in the suburbs, and for the first time in a long time, life for Kelsey was finally worth living.

"KELSEY, WAKE UP," TOM SAID THE MORNING AFTER a big storm. He playfully smacked her backside and grabbed some things from the floor.

"What is it?" Kelsey asked groggily.

Tom quickly moved about the room as he dressed himself in yesterday's clothes. "You're never going to believe this," he said, "but that storm last night did us a favor."

Kelsey breathed a sigh of relief. "It finally knocked down that old tree."

Tom shook his head. "Nope. The kids are already outside. Come see."

Her husband was out of the room before Kelsey could even get a yawn in. She stretched, popped her back, and sluggishly got out of bed. Then she dressed herself and went downstairs.

Her foot had just touched the bottom step when she heard it.

It was a sound she hadn't heard since she was twelve years old.

A flapping sound.

And it was coming from her backyard.

Kelsey advanced to the window, and her heart nearly sank to her feet when she saw pinwheeling colors fluttering outside.

"No...!"

Kelsey bolted for the back door and threw it open, just in time to find her husband and three children holding onto the parachute and raising it high above their heads.

"Look what the storm brought us, Mommy!" said her youngest son, Zachary.

"Can you believe it?" Tom said. "The wind just blew it here. It's not even ripped!"

The parachute ballooned toward the sky like a rippling cyst on the earth.

"Remember, guys," Tom called to the kids, "don't get caught!"

The parachute steadily floated down, and Zachary—smiling and laughing and barely able to walk in his dad's house slippers—stumbled underneath it.

The Candy Cane Man

"What the hell was that?"

"What was what?"

"Back there. I saw a face."

Hands on the steering wheel, Paul glanced in the rearview mirror and regarded the crumbling factory in its reflection. Painted on the factory's last remaining smokestack was what appeared to be a demonic baby licking a sharp candy cane.

"Oh, that's the old Sugar Baby Factory," Paul said. "They made candy back in the eighties."

In the passenger seat, Lee faced forward. "Why does the baby look so *evil?*"

Paul laughed. "Kids graffitied over it after the place caught fire. That factory doesn't have the best reputation around here. People think it's cursed."

"*What* people?" Lee scoffed.

Paul didn't want to admit it, but Lee was right. Geneva Grove was a ghost town.

The couple had spent the past five hours traveling from Lee's affluent two-bedroom apartment in Chicago to Paul's childhood home in Iowa. The tiny town didn't have any operating businesses or even a running post office, and it had been that way for years, but the skeletal remnants of its bygone era —remnants like the old Sugar Baby Factory—remained mostly intact.

"I don't understand how you grew up here," Lee remarked as the sedan turned onto what used to be Main Street. Two-story brick buildings flanked the road, but they were all empty and boarded up at the windows. Lee guessed if it weren't for the snow everywhere, he'd see tumbleweeds or old newspapers drifting in the wind.

"I got used to it," Paul said. "The hardest part was going to school. There wasn't one in town, so my grandmother had to drive me to the nearest city just so I could go."

"No schools," Lee observed. "I'm guessing this property isn't worth anything."

Paul soured at Lee's remark and stiffened his grip on the wheel. "I don't know. I wasn't planning on selling it."

"Why not?" Lee demanded. "I mean, you've already got a place with me—in a city that actually shows up on a GPS. What the hell are you going to do with an old shack in the middle of nowhere?"

"That *shack* is the house I grew up in," Paul corrected.

"It's also where your grandmother just died," Lee imparted, his tone almost as cold as the words themselves. "*And* it's where your mom overdosed when you were six. I'm not trying to be a dick, but why would you want to hang on to a house with memories like that?"

Paul agreed. Lee never tried to be a dick. Usually, he just *was* one.

"My grandmother raised me in that house, Lee. *She* was raised there." Lee knew all of this, so why did Paul have to repeat it now?

"All I'm saying is the past is the past," Lee said. "You should probably let it go."

Paul gritted his teeth. A memory of their most recent fight crawled through his mind like the scroll of a theater marquee. *You can't keep getting mad at me for an old mistake*, Lee had said after stepping out on him. *You need to let shit go.*

And Paul did let his mistake go—until Lee repeated it.

Again. And again.

You can let shit go, Paul realized, but sometimes shit holds on to you.

"I don't want to let go of the house," Paul said as the car turned onto a back road.

"Then what's your plan with it?" Lee asked. "I'm not moving here, if that's what you're thinking."

"Jesus, Lee, my grandmother's body isn't even cold yet. Can you lay off?"

Lee sunk into his seat and got quiet.

They sat in silence while Paul regarded his partner out of the corner of his eye.

It hadn't always been like this. For the first six months of their relationship, things had been great. Romantic dates. Practical jokes. Hopes for the future. It was why Paul felt comfortable enough to move in with Lee so quickly.

Now, not even a year later, the two could hardly carry a conversation that didn't end in conflict. Paul missed their reverence for each other. He would've given anything to get that spark back. But now, much like the town they currently inhabited, Paul understood and accepted that the spark between them was probably dead.

This town is where everything comes to die, he thought.

"*Why* is the factory cursed?" Lee asked suddenly.

Paul knew Lee wasn't going back to the previous conversation because he was interested in it. Lee was just doing what he always did—breaking the stoic silence he didn't want to endure.

"You said something about a fire," Lee pressed.

Paul was reluctant to elaborate. Lee didn't care about the factory, or the fire, or just about anything that didn't pertain to him directly. Paul didn't want to waste his breath on deaf ears, but talking about the factory—or anything else—was certainly better than fighting or sitting in an uncomfortable silence. Paul willingly took the bait.

"My grandfather used to work at the factory," Paul said. "He told the story to my grandmother, and then she passed it on to me. Anyway, the story goes, these kids snuck into the factory over their Christmas break and lit some firecrackers. It was supposed to be a prank to scare the workers, but something went wrong."

Lee hit the button for the seat warmers. Paul wasn't sure if he was listening but continued with the story.

"One of the workers was so startled by the firecrackers, he accidentally caught his hands in the batch roller used to make candy canes. The cylinders pulled him into the machine and completely mangled him."

The snow was coming down hard, dusting the windshield like a powdered cookie. Paul flicked the toggle for the wipers, and the blades scraped across the glass with such quickness, he thought he saw Lee jump in his seat.

"The workers—many of them being relatives of the kids— didn't want to see their lives ruined over one mistake. So they lit the place up, told investigators there was a sugar dust explosion, and everything was swept under the rug."

"That's fucked up," Lee declared.

"Not as fucked up as what happened *after* the fire," Paul continued. "One by one, the kids responsible for that man's death went missing—vanished from their homes in the middle of the night, never to be seen again. Then the factory workers disappeared, too. Eventually, *everyone* in Geneva Grove started to vanish. Police couldn't figure out what was going on or who was responsible. There was only one thing collected from each victim's home that offered any sort of clue—a calling card, if you will."

"What was it?"

Paul raised his hand and curled his index finger into the shape of a hook. "A candy cane hanging from their front door."

Paul waited for Lee to say something, but he didn't. He seemed to hang on to every word, more interested in the story than Paul initially gave him credit for.

"That's why everyone became superstitious and left this town," Paul concluded. "No one wanted to fall victim to the curse. No one wanted to be taken by...*the Candy Cane Man.*"

Paul moaned like a ghoul and prodded Lee with his hooked finger.

Lee was less than amused. He huffed and turned his gaze to the window.

Paul's smile faded. Six months ago, Lee would've been tickled by the story. He would've brushed it off with a nervous laugh, gently slugged him on the arm, called him a goddamn idiot, or even pretended to see a ghost on the side of the road to scare Paul back.

Instead, Lee stared out the window and said nothing. Now they were back to the uncomfortable silence both so desperately wanted to avoid.

The car made a right turn, and the couple bounced in their seats as the road beneath them gave way to rocky gravel. Moments later, they could see the silhouette of a small cottage sitting alone in a snow-covered field, awaiting them at the end of the long driveway.

"Home, sweet home," Paul announced.

They had arrived.

———

IF THE DRIVE TO IOWA HAD BEEN UNCOMFORTABLE, then their stay in the old house was emphatically unbearable.

Lee complained before the couple had even walked through the front door. First, it was about the home's curb appeal, or lack thereof. Lee addressed each of the home's shortcomings, from its sagging gutters to its crumbling asbestos siding.

Then, once they were inside the house, Lee's negativity shifted from depleted to fully pessimistic.

"This place is a dump," he growled, blowing into his hands for warmth. "Does the heat even work?"

Paul tried his best to disregard Lee's skepticism, but his partner's harsh words had already burrowed under his skin like the proboscis of a bloodthirsty mosquito. "I'll check the thermostat."

Lee's eyes rolled in their sockets before settling on the room around him.

Much like its former occupant, the living room was small and antiquated. In the corner was a six-foot artificial Christmas tree adorned with tinsel and handblown glass ornaments. A textured sofa with fraying fibers sat next to it, facing an even older console television that looked less like an electronic and more like a piece of furniture.

Lee fumbled with one of the TV knobs, unsure how to work the stupid thing, then gave up and smacked it in defeat. He glanced at the gold-plated picture frame sitting atop the television set where a black-and-white photo of Paul's grandmother smiled back at him.

"Thanks for nothing, Grams," he said.

The old woman's eyes seemed to follow Lee as he headed for the kitchen, which was hardly an improvement over the living room. The yellowed appliances and chipped cabinets appeared to be original to the home. The kitchen table was wobbly and decorated with water rings. The only thing that seemed to work like new was the Earl Arnault–inspired Kit-Cat Klock that ticked loudly from the far wall, its swinging black tail and volleying eyes clacking with each passing second.

Lee begrudgingly made his way deeper into the house, only to discover the bedrooms and single bathroom matching the quality of the rest of it. The bathroom was so small, he was sure it could only hold one person at a time, and the two bedrooms were so tightly packed with old furniture, there was hardly room to walk around the beds.

Twin beds, Lee noticed.

"Guess we'll be sleeping in separate rooms," Paul said, suddenly standing behind Lee, who jumped at the sound of his voice. Paul elbowed Lee's side with a strap-up-your-boots smile. The nudge was playful, and his smile as genuine as ever, but Lee didn't share in Paul's optimism.

"We're not sleeping here," Lee said.

"I didn't plan to," Paul replied, going to the window and looking outside. "But the snow's really coming down out there. I don't think we have a choice."

"We're not sleeping here," Lee said again, hoping that by repeating himself, Paul would inexplicably jump onto Lee's train of thought and change his mind.

"The nearest hotel is forty minutes away," Paul divulged, the crooks of his smile disappearing. "It's getting dark. I'm sorry, but I just don't think it's safe to drive."

Lee licked his lips, his eyes bouncing back and forth like the clock in the kitchen. He stuck to his guns and extended an arm. "Give me your keys."

"What?"

"If you won't drive me out of this nightmare, I'll do it myself."

"Come on, babe. It's been a long day. We're both tired. The heat's working now, so let's just sleep here tonight, and in the morning, we'll meet with the lawyer—"

"No, Paul! You said we would check out the house for a bit and then head to a hotel. I'm not sleeping in this fucking shed because of a few snowflakes or because *you* want to reminisce! I want your keys—now!"

Lee's stare was as hard as stone.

Paul opened his mouth to respond but thought better of it. He was unsurprised by his partner but still disheartened. He knew there was no convincing him.

Digging into his jeans pocket, Paul fished out his keys and tossed them to Lee, who grabbed them against his chest with a staggered look on his face.

"There's a Super 8 in Williams," Paul said flatly.

Then he walked away.

———

Lee's grip on the steering wheel was as tight as his convictions. He rested his heavy leg on the gas pedal with no proclivity to relieve it.

The white sedan drummed over a cattle guard as it bounded down the snow-covered gravel road, coming over the horizon like a tiny monster on wheels. The pitiful sound of the two-cylinder engine barely stood a chance against the wind's ghostly howl.

The snow fell with an unrivaled insistence and rare intensity. Flocculent clumps of ice stuck to the vehicle's wipers as they thumped back and forth.

Leaning close to the steering column, Lee squinted his eyes, trying to see through the foggy windshield without success. He attempted to clear the inside of the glass with his hand, and when that failed, he blindly batted at the instrument cluster to turn up the heat. His eyes strayed to the temperature knobs, allowing the vehicle a split-second moment to jerk out of his hands and veer to the left. Lee reacted quickly, righting the wheel and regaining control of the car.

Lee tried to keep his focus on the road, but it was difficult with Paul's words replaying in his mind.

"Let's just sleep here," Lee mock-mumbled to himself, his red face in stark contrast to the snow outside. *"Let's just stay here forever and weave baskets and chop firewood and shuck corn—"*

Outside, the gray sky deepened into an inky and starless black.

"—we can milk our own cows, slaughter our own chickens, start a religion, sacrifice a fucking goat—"

Lee laughed at the absurdity of it all. Did Paul really think he was going to manipulate him like that? Was he out of his goddamn mind?

Lee glimpsed the road ahead—what he could see of it, anyway—and stomped the brake. The car slid for a moment before the tires found their grip with the earth and brought the vehicle to a halt.

"What the—?"

Opening the door, Lee stuck his head out of the car, just to be sure he was seeing what he thought he was seeing.

There was a fallen tree in the road.

The tree stretched crosswise over the snowy gravel like a makeshift bridge over an icy river. A dusting of snow had already collected on top of its trunk, reminding Lee of the sugary glaze on a vanilla eclair.

"You gotta be fucking kidding me," he said through clenched teeth.

Lee shivered against the wind and surveyed the scene. He looked at the wide-open Iowan fields, wondering how this tree —the only tree in the entire field as far as he could see—just happened to fall immediately after their arrival and across Lee's only path back to the real world.

His only *escape*.

Lee thought of veering the car off the gravel road and going around the tree, but he couldn't see the ground under the snow. As far as he knew, the sides of the road were rocky trenches, and he didn't feel comfortable blindly driving over possibly treacherous land in an economy car burdened with front-wheel drive.

He thought of moving the tree himself, but even with his athletic build, he knew he didn't have the manpower.

He considered using the car to pull the tree out of the way, but with what? It wasn't like Paul kept chains under the seats for this sort of thing. And even if he did, Lee wasn't sure how to attach the chains to the car and was likely to rip the bumper off.

More than anything, Lee thought about returning to that godforsaken house and seeing the shit-eating grin on Paul's face when he walked through the door.

That particular thought fueled his rage.

"Fuck!"

With no other choice, Lee dropped into his seat and shut the door.

The car did a three-point-turn and journeyed back to the house.

———

PAUL WASN'T WAITING FOR LEE WITH A SHIT-EATING grin on his face.

He wasn't waiting at all.

It appeared Paul had already sequestered himself in one of the bedrooms for the night. Lee assumed his partner was trying to avoid him just as much as Lee was trying to avoid Paul, and that was perfectly fine. With the way he was feeling, Lee was satisfied if he *never* saw Paul again.

Still, he let out a sigh as he scoped out the remaining bedroom, a space that hardly seemed big enough to accommodate his exaggerated breath, let alone the entirety of his six-foot frame.

The bed was timeworn with a single purple-brown stain in the middle of the patchwork quilt. Lee imagined the quilt being draped over Paul's lifeless grandmother before being returned to the bed, *unwashed*, and he felt his skin crawl at the prospect. Lee knew the old woman had died from a fall, but Paul never specified *where* on the property the fall had occurred.

Did she die in the house? Lee wondered. Did she die in this room?

He'd never know with Paul remaining so aloof.

Lee considered texting Paul to find out where his grandmother had met her demise, at least before committing to a place to rest his head for the night, but the possibility of his text going unread, or worse, *read with no reply*, kept that thought from becoming anything more than a consideration.

If there was any clout in maintaining control of the relationship—and of Paul—it was Lee's intention to keep it all for himself.

Fuck Paul, he decided.

And fuck this bed, too.

———

Lee couldn't sleep. The archaic couch in the living room was so uncomfortable that he could feel two rusty springs poking through the upholstery and stabbing him in the back. The sharp points spiraled into his shoulder blades like a vampire taking a bite out of him. Lee rolled onto his side for some relief, and as he did, the springs recoiled and jabbed him in the ribs. It was as if the couch had made a bad joke and was nudging him to laugh.

Outside, the wind raged, but the old house flexed against it and proved a strong asylum. The walls of the home groaned in battle.

The noise of it all was insufferable. Lee grabbed the throw pillow from under his cheek and clapped it to his exposed ear. It was a fruitless effort as the sounds slipped through the stuffing and continued their assault on him.

Finally, he'd had enough. Lee dismissed the idea of sleep and sat up. Between the painful couch and the noise outside, sleep was a castle in the air.

Lee made to grab his phone from the armrest when the front door blew open. A gust of wind carried a cloud of flurries into the front entryway as the door swung all the way back and punched a hole in the wall.

Hastening to close the door, Lee jumped up and twisted his feet around the legs of the coffee table, narrowly catching his balance against the wall. The moment of clumsiness gave him the auspicious instant to see something on the front door he hadn't noticed before.

There was a candy cane hanging from the outside doorknob.

Lee stood in place for a moment, watching the candy cane lightly swing back and forth like the pendulum of a grandfather clock.

Lee's eyes drifted to the open doorway. He listened with intent, trying to isolate the sound of someone outside, possibly fleeing across the snow or perhaps even hiding in the darkness, but there was nothing to be heard over the unruly wind.

He stepped closer to the threshold and flipped a switch. The dark porch was suddenly bathed in incandescent light.

No one was there.

Lee looked down, expecting to see a fresh trail of footprints leading away from the house, maybe even tire tracks of some kind, but as far as he could see, the blanket of snow on the ground was smooth and undisturbed.

Whoever put the candy cane on the door must've been floating in the air, he thought.

Or maybe they were already in the house and had hooked it from inside.

Lee narrowed his eyes as the realization struck him.

Paul.

Lee palmed the front door, swung it shut, and angrily crossed to the back bedroom to confront his partner.

"You're a fucking ass—!" was all Lee managed to get out before he threw open the door and was confronted with an empty bedroom.

"Paul?"

Lee flicked on the light for a better look, but there was no trickery. Paul wasn't in the room.

In confused alarm, Lee investigated the other bedroom, surprised to find it empty as well.

He checked the bathroom next, recalling Paul getting up once or twice in the middle of the night to take a piss.

Paul wasn't there.

As far as Lee could tell, Paul wasn't *anywhere.*

He's hiding and waiting to jump out at me, Lee convinced himself. All for a stupid prank. All so he can get even.

With that conviction, Lee stood tall and shouted, "Enough, Paul! I'm not falling for your bullshit games! Come on out!"

When silence was the only reply, Lee let out a frustrated breath and began to think. He remembered Paul always keeping his phone's ringer volume up, so if Lee could just call him, the sound of his ringtone might reveal his whereabouts.

But when Lee made his way back to the living room to grab his phone, another surprise awaited him.

His phone was gone.

Lee's face muscles tightened. Somehow, the missing phone felt like a more personal attack on him than his own life partner disappearing. Lee's confused irritation quickly turned to blind rage.

"Where's my fucking phone?!" he shouted, throwing pillows and couch cushions aside, hoping the device had just slipped into the crevices of the furniture.

When his desperate reaction turned up zero results, Lee marched toward the kitchen, ready to ransack that space next. He knew his tantrum was unlikely to bring him any closer to his phone, but in the heat of the moment, taking his aggression out on a house he so fervently hated was enough to temporarily assuage his fury.

As he approached the kitchen, Lee stopped dead in his tracks.

It was too dark to be sure, but he thought he saw the figure of an old woman drift past the kitchen entryway.

"H-hello?" he called out.

Lee stood in place, waiting for whoever was there to respond or reappear.

Then there was a sound behind him.

Lee whipped around, surprised to find the front door blown open once again.

No. Not blown open.

While the door was indeed ajar, there were no gusts of wind assaulting the entryway—no sounds of combat as the house stood its ground against Mother Nature.

The wind outside had stopped completely.

Lee stepped closer to the open door and gazed outside, staring beyond the glow of the porch light and into the shadowed abyss.

Something in the darkness stared back at him with wide, yellow eyes.

Lee froze, unsure of what he was seeing but assured it was there just the same.

There was someone standing in the field—not the old woman he thought he saw in the kitchen, but a man, taller than a doorway and wearing a gray pinstriped coverall and fiddler's cap.

There was something peculiar about the man, a strangeness that made Lee believe the man wasn't really a man at all, but something else completely.

Something inhuman.

Some...*thing*.

The man's arms were impossibly long, so elongated that his limbs didn't rest at his sides but instead touched the ground in front of him, extending outward like forearm crutches. At the end of each arm was a broken wrist that curved upward like the hook of a shepherd's crook.

But it was the man's hands Lee noticed most of all, or lack thereof. Where his hands should've been were twisted knobs of bone, viscera, and peppermint candy that had been sharpened into deadly spikes.

Lee thought of the Sugar Baby Factory mascot—of the infant sucking on a candy cane until it had sharpened it into a fine point—and felt the color leave his face.

The creature that wasn't a man hunched over and took a step toward the house, using its deformed arms as hiking canes. Each hooked limb stabbed into the snow as it pulled itself forward.

Lee hesitantly stepped back from the open door, unsure of what to do, unsure of how to react.

Was this part of Paul's prank? Lee wondered. Was this just some elaborate disguise Paul had concocted to scare him? It would certainly be out of character for Paul, but not totally impossible.

The inhuman thing opened its mouth, and its jaw practically fell to its chest as it let out a primal screech—a monstrous, gravelly cry that sounded as if its throat was coated with crushed bits of candy finally coming loose.

Lee knew it wasn't Paul, and it wasn't a prank.

Whatever the thing was, it was real.

The thing suddenly lurched forward, coming across the snow like a hungry mantis chasing a housefly. Its heavy arms punched the ground as it closed the gap between itself and the house faster than Lee could process what was happening.

Lee jumped back and swung the front door shut, but the dangling candy cane shifted on the knob and prevented the door from clicking into place. The door bounced off the hard candy stick and drifted back open.

The thing swiftly skulked up the front porch. It extended a hooked arm into the house and fished for its prey.

Lee dodged the reaching limb and fell back. He managed to crawl to the other side of the room when a surge of pain exploded in his leg. He glanced back, horrified to see the thing's hook buried in his thigh. It had sliced into his flesh as easily as a meat thermometer sliding into a perfectly cooked roast.

Fraught to rid himself of the hook, Lee thrashed and clawed and raked his fingers across the hardwood floor, but he was as hopeless as a snared fox at the mercy of its hunter.

Lee turned over onto his back, and the thing's second hook came barreling down on him, right into his face. The spiky point caught Lee in his gaping mouth, hooking into his lower jaw and erupting from the soft patch of skin under his chin. An explosion of red splattered the floor.

The pain was excruciating. Lee tried to scream, but the hook blocked his capacity to do so.

Blood pooled over Lee's face as the thing gruffly jerked him across the room and dragged him outside. Lee's body thumped across the porch and into the driveway, moving across the icy snow and away from the ramshackle house—a house that looked less like a dumpy shed and more like the happiest place on earth.

The last thing Lee saw before the blood took his vision was someone standing on the front porch of the house and removing the candy cane from the doorknob—the candy cane that, according to Paul's story, should've been left behind as a calling card.

The candy cane that had actually lured the creature out of dormancy and was no longer needed.

The figure on the porch opened the candy stick, sucked on it, and appeared to wave as the creature dragged Lee away, across the snowy fields to depths unknown, to a realm of unspeakable horror yet to be experienced.

———

THE CANDY CANE RESTED IN THE CORNER OF PAUL'S mouth like a tobacco pipe as he watched his grandfather haul his partner away. Paul waved again, hoping his grandfather had noticed the gesture but accepting he'd never know just the same. Either way, Paul was just happy to see him.

Lee's cries faded to nothing as he was pulled over the horizon. He and the creature disappeared into the darkness, and as they did, the wind abruptly returned.

Paul took his time finishing the candy cane before finally pocketing his hands and going inside.

He didn't jump or scream when he saw the old woman sitting on the couch. Instead, he sat next to his grandmother, joining her to watch a *Merrie Melodies* cartoon about a mouse trying to stay up all night to see Santa Claus. He remembered watching the same Christmas special many times as a kid. It was his routine safe space whenever his grandmother performed the ritual of the candy cane. Now that it was *his* turn to pull the strings, he smiled at the idea of his grandmother occupying her time with the same thing he used to do. It felt like a circle being completed.

"How do you feel?" the old woman asked.

He didn't answer right away because he was feeling many things. He was excited for getting the chance to see his grandfather again. He felt accomplished for successfully completing the ritual—and relief for effectively blindsiding Lee and never having to put up with his toxic narcissism ever again.

But, somewhere in the dark recesses of Paul's conscience, he was feeling a little guilty, and for someone with a past as disconcerting as his, that was more than a little alarming.

Paul recalled his mother feeling remorseful after she performed the candy cane ritual on his good-for-nothing father. Paul remembered coming home about a month after his father's disappearance and finding his mother facedown on the bed in a puddle of her own vomit, an empty pill bottle in her hand. No matter how much his abusive father deserved what happened to him, the guilt his mother faced in the aftermath of her decision was just too much for her to bear.

Those were hard times in their lives, and Paul knew his grandmother worried a similar circumstance could occur now. But Paul was adamant not to let the guilt cloud his mind, and he didn't dare speak of these feelings to his grandmother. He swore to never put her through that pain ever again.

"I feel great," he finally answered. "I got to see Grandpa."

The old woman offered a small smile.

"Did you get to see him?" he asked.

She shook her head, disappointed. "Not this year."

"Maybe next Christmas," Paul assured her.

"Maybe," she agreed.

Neither one knew it, but they were both already thinking —like addicts seeking a fix—of who would get the candy cane next.

Monstrous

Reed was halfway across the Hiltzik River Bridge when he saw the dog. He was video chatting with his social media manager, Trish, and noticed the Border Collie lying on the deck near one of the steel gusset plates. He thought the dog would see him and at least wag its tail, so he was surprised when the canine locked eyes with him and didn't move a muscle.

"Are you listening, Reed?" Trish huffed from the phone screen. It was difficult to hear her over the sound of the rushing water below, but Reed knew she was still going on about his declining viewership and waning followers.

"I hear you, Trish," Reed said and didn't expound any further. They both understood why he was losing followers so quickly, and he noticed Trish trying especially hard not to vocalize it. She was tiptoeing around the subject the way Reed was tiptoeing past the dog.

"We need to fix this," Trish said. "*You* need to fix this."

"What do you want me to say?" Reed asked defensively. "One day, the world loves you; the next, you're canceled. There isn't a science to this shit."

"Oh, but there *is* a science to it," Trish refuted. "I've spent my entire adult life studying social media and online trends. I have a master's in digital audiences for a reason."

That's a thing? Reed wanted to say but chose to bite his tongue.

"Look, Reed, you're never going to get out of this deep shit you're in if you don't address what's happening. You either need to publicly defend your character against these...*allegations*—" She spat the word out as if it were a piece of gristle. "—or you need to concede to the rumor mill and own up to what you did. Whatever you do, you're gonna have to show some vulnerability if you want the world to be on your side again."

She was right, but for Reed, hearing the truth from someone he trusted didn't make it any easier to digest.

Reed finally crossed to the other side of the truss bridge, glancing back at the dog once more. He took particular notice of the animal's matted fur and concave ribs, and it made him think of his own dog back at home and the condition the animal had been in when Reed first found him.

It was the summer of 2018, and Reed and his girlfriend, Jessica, had gone ATV-riding with some friends. The foursome took a trip to Montgomery County, where a group of property investors and their crew had already bulldozed over fifty acres of woods to build a new strip mall. With the land mostly leveled, the area had temporarily become the perfect place for four-wheeling.

It was a scenic day, hotter than usual but bearable in the steady breeze. The group spent an hour enjoying the mounds and off-camber trails when they decided to take a break from the heat and cool off with some beers. They shut off the engines, and that's when they could hear whimpering from somewhere nearby.

Upon investigating the sound, they discovered a small Beagle trapped in a ten-inch-wide crevice near one of the hills. From the looks of its gaunt frame, the scared and helpless animal had been stuck at the bottom of the trench for at least a few days.

Reed was the first to spring into action. He tried to grab the dog, but the animal was too far down to reach. While the others joined him in his effort and contemplated a plan to get the dog out, Jessica stood to the side, grabbed her boyfriend's iPhone, and started recording.

First, the group widened the crevice by digging outward with some nearby rocks. Then two of them held Reed's ankles as he got onto his stomach, wedged his upper body into the gap, and wiggled his way down. When Reed was able to reach the dog, he grabbed it by the scruff and called for the others to pull him up. The group heaved Reed to the surface, and the frightened dog came with him in one fell swoop.

Reed and Jessica took the animal to a vet, who determined the dog was a two-year-old male and most likely a stray. The dog was lucky he didn't have any critical injuries from the fall, but still, because of his malnourishment, the clinic decided to keep him until he was back to normal levels. In no time at all, the dog had completed his recovery, and with some extra weight on his bones and a clean bill of health, he was microchipped, given the name Dirt, and taken to his forever home with Reed and Jessica.

It was Jessica who encouraged Reed to upload the video of the rescue to Facebook. She insisted it would be something good for the two of them to see later in Reed's "memories." Neither of them conceived the video gaining an audience in the tens of millions and being shared around the world.

When the video went viral, Reed couldn't wrap his head around his newfound celebrity, or why people were so enamored by him specifically. After all, there were hundreds—if not *thousands*—of animal rescue videos posted online every day. What made his video so special?

"It's because you're hot," Jessica told him as the video continued to gain traction. "Everyone likes seeing a hot guy be the hero."

Reed didn't see himself that way. Sure, he had a handsome face and a nice body, but whenever he looked at himself in the mirror, he mostly saw a guy who was twenty-nine, who had never gone to college, and had worked his entire adult life in a garage—a job he never liked and wasn't particularly proud of. Reed hardly saw himself as a catch. How he was able to snag the attention of a beautiful girl like Jessica, he never knew.

When the video took off and awarded Reed an unanticipated fifteen minutes of fame, he saw it as a means of changing his life for the better. Reed knew he needed to extend those fifteen minutes into something more substantial but wasn't entirely sure how. He had merely saved an animal in need by being in the right place at the right time—and apparently looking good doing it. What monetary value was there in that?

He didn't have to wait long to find out.

A week after the video was posted—and the day it hit its ten millionth view on Facebook alone—a producer from Good Morning America got in touch with Reed and invited him to be a guest on the show, and that was a start. They offered to pay for his and Jessica's flight, their four-star hotel, and Reed's time for doing the show. He gladly accepted. Contracts were signed, and two days later, he and Jessica were on a flight to New York City in first-class seats.

Reed was nervous about the interview but carried himself remarkably well. Being a good-looking guy with a heavy Southern drawl, he was quick to charm the hosts (and the audience) with his likable, relatable, and even goofy personality.

But it's what happened at the end of the interview that changed everything.

Just as the hosts were wrapping things up, a bird that had somehow snuck into the studio flew down from the rafters. It flapped around the audience and hit one of the cameras, startling one of the hosts right out of her chair.

When the exhausted bird finally landed on the floor of the stage, Reed—in perfect composure—calmly got up from his seat, took off his shirt, and gently placed it over the panicked vertebrate. Then he scooped up the bird and handed it to the nearest production assistant for safe keeping.

As the crowd fawned over Reed's chiseled body and naturally tanned skin, someone in the audience shouted, "Rescue Reed! Rescue Reed!"

The chant quickly caught on, and soon it was a song echoed by hundreds of people throughout the studio, and by the end of the day, it was a hashtag trending across all social media.

It was in that moment the world was smitten, and "Rescue Reed" was born.

Within a day, Reed's followers on Instagram alone went from an adequate seven hundred to a staggering sixty thousand. He received hundreds of messages from people all over the world, mostly sent by single women and lusting gay men hoping to snag his attention. Reed and Jessica shared a flattered laugh about the virtual hubbub, but some of the messages proved unexpectedly promising. The owner of a pet store asked him to make an appearance at an adoption event, and a movie producer invited him to the red-carpet premiere of some animated film about talking pets. At Jessica's insistence, he happily agreed to both.

The online messages and offers continued, doubling within days, tripling within weeks, and becoming so overwhelming by the end of the month, Reed wasn't sure he could read each message, let alone respond to any of them.

That's when Jessica mentioned Trish, whom she knew from high school and understood was proficient in marketing and the business side of social media.

"Do whatever Trish tells you," Jessica advised, "and you'll be as good as gold."

Jessica was right, and by working on his brand of "Rescue Reed," Trish catapulted Reed's fifteen minutes of fame into a career he never thought possible.

Trish was able to secure a permanent engagement for Reed at a local animal shelter called Nothin' but a Pound Dog. His position was to work with new animals and make them feel as comfortable in the shelter as possible. He was even given permission to film his time with the animals for his social media accounts. Nothin' but a Pound Dog became so heavily trafficked with people wanting to see Reed, it started to feel less like a place of work and more like the venue of his unofficial meet-and-greet. The organization never saw his celebrity as a problem, as they didn't hold on to any of their animals for very long—not with the mere promise of families getting the chance to meet Reed just by showing an interest in adopting.

Then came the brand deals with PetSmart, Purina, and Blue Buffalo. Reed couldn't believe how much money could be made by simply taking a photo or video of a product and sharing it to social media—not to mention all the free stuff he could give to Dirt back home.

Finally, and perhaps most importantly, Trish was able to get permission for Reed to assist animal control groups in their rescues. This became the perfect means for Reed to film and post more brand-specific content. He rescued dogs from sewer gutters, cats from trees, and various farm animals from barbed-wire fences. At first, Jessica was able to accompany Reed on his excursions, serving as Reed's private camerawoman. But when

Animal Planet expressed an interest in filming a pilot about Reed and his rescues, everything changed.

The pilot became the most-watched program in the channel's history, catapulting Reed from social media influencer to worldwide superstar. A twelve-episode series was greenlit, and Reed found himself traveling the country with a professional film crew who, by no ill will of their own, had become his new family and replaced the role initially held by his longtime girlfriend.

With Reed's financial permanence, Jessica was able to quit her job as a cashier and stay home, something Reed assumed his girlfriend would love. But for Jessica, being by herself with no one to talk to only made her feel lonely and dejected. She tried occupying her time playing with Dirt and focusing on her own hobbies, but Jessica still felt like she was missing out on something she believed she was partially responsible for. If she hadn't recorded Dirt's rescue and encouraged Reed to share it with the world, she wondered if she would be feeling so ostracized being stuck at home by herself. The money and notoriety were nice, but she missed having a partner in life who was physically there to share in life's experiences.

When Reed wasn't home, he was filming. When he wasn't filming, he was promoting. And when his breakout show was renewed for a second season, Reed and Jessica saw less of each other than ever before.

On the nights he wasn't home, Reed and his production crew stayed in hotels. Reed would settle into his own room and call Jessica on the phone, filling her in on his day's events but always forgetting to ask about her own.

One evening, Jessica finally broke down and cried, telling him how forgotten and disposable she felt—how she hardly believed she had a boyfriend anymore with how little they saw of each other and how infrequently he would ask how *she* was doing. This led to their first fight in years, the two eventually screaming and yelling and hanging up without resolution.

Instead of calling her back, Reed went downstairs to the hotel bar and started a tab. He figured if he couldn't resolve the conflict with Jessica, he could at least settle the throbbing in his skull with some Tennessee Whiskey. He couldn't understand how Jessica could be so ungrateful after everything he'd worked for. Sure, Jessica had a point that Reed was constantly busy and always on the move, but didn't she recognize he was doing it all for the *both* of them?

Reed was on his fourth drink when the beautiful stranger with the blonde hair and tight-fitting shirt recognized him from across the bar. The woman joined Reed for a drink and fawned over him, flirtatiously touching his thigh as she recalled how sexy he looked on his show—and how much sexier he was in person. Her perfectly manicured hand found its way up his leg, to the noticeable bulge of his jeans, a part of his body he astutely realized hadn't been touched by anyone but himself in months. The stranger's touch and attention felt good, and in less than an hour, Reed had succumbed to the sauce and his weak inhibitions, and the two were sneaking upstairs and fucking in his bed.

When Reed awoke the next morning, he thought the woman would be gone or, at the very least, dressing to leave. He was surprised to find her still lying next to him, awake and wearing his flannel shirt, her iPhone raised above her face as if she were taking a selfie. He realized the woman was broadcasting a LIVE video of the two of them, and in that moment, Reed knew his life was about to change—again.

TMZ first reported the affair, followed by every news channel and notable social media outlet. Reed's name and brand were trending more than ever, and despite his efforts, word of the affair reached Jessica before Reed ever could. He called her and tried to apologize, telling her everything he thought she would want to hear, but his labors were useless. Jessica was done with him, and their seven-year relationship was over.

But Jessica wasn't the only one finished with Reed. In spite of his show's tremendous success, Animal Planet decided to cut their losses and pull the plug on the new season. Due to the bad publicity, all of Reed's sponsors ended their relationship with him. Reed was no longer welcomed to provide his assistance on any animal rescue cases, and Nothin' but a Pound Dog wrote him off without so much as a thank you for all he had done for the organization.

One bad decision, and everything was gone.

He was reminded of an expression his father used to say throughout his childhood: "Reed, you can get ninety-nine 'atta boys,' but people will only remember you for one 'aw, shit.'"

This was Reed's "aw, shit"—and it had cost him everything he cherished most in his life.

All that was left was Trish, still on the phone with Reed as he stepped off the Hiltzik River Bridge and onto the next path through Arawak Park. Trish wondered if it was even worth the effort to save Reed's career—if he even *deserved* to be saved after what he did to Jessica. Ultimately, Trish decided to remain loyal to him, not because she forgave or sympathized with him, but simply because it felt unprofessional to walk away.

"What are you going to do, Reed?" she asked.

"It doesn't matter," he said to her. "Did you see the comments on that article? People are accusing me of all kinds of shit." He was ready to list the horrible things people had been saying about him—how they accused him of sleeping with someone at Animal Planet to get his show; how he even staged some of the animal rescues just so he'd have something to film!

"I saw the comments," Trish answered.

"So you know I'm the bad guy," Reed said, less with defeat and more with a pathetic acceptance. "It's been decided for me. I'll be the bad guy for the rest of my life. There's no changing it."

"You're *not* a bad guy," Trish said, even if she didn't fully believe it herself. "You just need to remind the world of the good you're capable of."

Reed rolled his eyes. The more the world accused him of terrible things, the less good he wanted to do for the world.

This is how villains are made, he thought.

Then his thoughts pivoted, and he wondered if Trish was right. Maybe Reed *could* remind his followers of who he was before the affair. Maybe if he kept his efforts and virtual presence on rescuing animals, he wouldn't need to address any of the controversy at all.

Don't feed the trolls, he thought.

But how was he going to rescue any animals without a team of people to help him find animals in need?

It was then he remembered the dog he saw on the bridge.

The Border Collie with the matted fur and concave ribs.

The animal he was suddenly sure would solve all his problems.

"I gotta go," Reed told Trish and abruptly ended the call.

Reed ran back to the bridge, more than confident the stray would still be in the same spot as where he had left it.

It wasn't.

Reed panicked, but only for a moment, surmising the animal couldn't have gotten far in its fragile condition.

This time, he was right.

The dog had only moved from the bridge to the riverbank. It walked slowly and quietly as it advanced to the water for a much-needed drink.

Reed checked his surroundings and found he was the only

person in the park. He looked up and regarded the overcast sky, reasoning the approaching storm having something to do with the lack of people around.

If there was somebody else in the park, Reed might have asked them to hold his phone for him—"It's already recording"—while he delicately approached the dog and earned its trust. Because he was alone, Reed elected to prop his phone against a tree instead, angling the camera lens toward the river and hoping for the best.

The dog was still drinking when Reed began his approach. He moved slowly, trying not to make a sound and risk scaring the animal away. It was when Reed had cleared most of the gap between himself and the dog that the canine finally detected his presence and turned around. Reed could mentally conjure the sound of the dog's neck muscles creaking as it struggled to raise its head. It acknowledged Reed with a small nod and regarded him with melancholy eyes.

"Hey, buddy," Reed said, stepping closer and holding out one hand for the dog to sniff. "It's okay. I'm not gonna hurt you."

The dog took in Reed's scent, keeping its head low and tail tucked between its legs.

"You don't have to be afraid," Reed said with a smile as he crouched down. "I'm your friend. I want to help you."

The dog licked his hand and moved closer, nuzzling its head into Reed's chest. Reed petted the animal and scratched behind its ears. The dog finally wagged its tail.

"What do you say we get outta here? You wanna come with me?"

The dog licked his face, and Reed smiled.

"I'll take that as a yes."

Reed worried that when he picked up the dog, he might aggravate a spot of tenderness somewhere, prompting the animal to lash out and bite him. He was grateful the dog allowed him to scoop it up, and he was even more thankful it didn't show any signs of pain or discomfort being in his arms.

"There you go," Reed said soothingly and started the walk back to his phone. "Let's get you cleaned up, huh?"

Reed was feeling good as he navigated back to the tree, but as he looked at his recording phone waiting in the distance, he started having doubts about what he was doing. Reed now had footage of himself gaining the dog's trust, but what was he supposed to do with it? Compile the footage with clips of the dog riding in his car? Taking a bath? Eating treats? Playing fetch?

He thought of those lengthy before-and-after rescue videos a website like The Dodo would often share. Reed knew he could create something similar, but no matter how good he was at editing something together, he didn't have time to waste on that.

Reed needed to post something today.

Something that was going to distract the world from the awful thing he did.

Something big.

And there was nothing BIG about this—nothing that was going to grab the world's attention the way his first video had.

Reed thought of that video now—of Dirt being trapped, helpless, and scared—and recognized that was the difference.

This dog wasn't trapped.

This dog wasn't helpless.

And while it certainly acted anxious, this dog wasn't exactly scared.

Reed was helping the dog, that was true, but was he actually *rescuing* it?

He looked at the dog in his arms, who had become restless and was squirming to get free.

Reed let the dog drop. It hit the ground a little harder than he had intended before sulking back to the rushing waters of the Hiltzik River.

The river.

No one would care if the dog was found roaming the open grounds of a public park.

But if Reed rescued the dog from the *river*...

"No," Reed said aloud as he shook away the intrusive thought. That wouldn't be right. The dog had probably been through more in the last week than Reed had been through in his entire life. The poor thing didn't deserve to be forced into the river for the sake of a viral video. That was exactly what the trolls of the internet were falsely accusing him of.

All the more reason to do it, the little red devil on Reed's shoulder advised. *People already believe it's true. Now you'll have someone to blame for putting the idea in your head when you get caught.*

If you get caught, Reed thought next.

He looked around the park again. Not a soul for miles.

Who would catch him?

Reed accepted that maybe it wouldn't be as awful as he imagined. After all, people push each other into lakes and swimming pools to be funny all the time. This wouldn't be much different from that—right?

It was this thought that made up his mind, and Reed was unfaltering in his decision to follow through with it.

Reed's gaze drifted to the dog shuffling along the river-bank, then settled on the bridge. He decided the best angle to record the scene would be directly from the top of the bridge, overlooking the river below. The setup was simple. After readying his phone camera, he'd toss the dog over one side of the bridge—against the flow of the current. When the dog drifted under the bridge and reemerged from the other side, Reed would take off his shirt, jump in after it, and bring the animal to the sandbar. He'd give it lots of worried attention and TLC, really phoning it in that saving the dog was miraculous timing and an unexpected act of bravery. He'd edit it all later for time and content.

Reed was surprised how easy it all seemed, and he was quite pleased with himself.

This was going to work, he thought.

How could it not?

Setting up the camera was easy, and reapproaching the dog and picking it up again wasn't much of a challenge. The dog fidgeted in Reed's arms as he carried it to the bridge, but hardly enough to make the undertaking a struggle.

There was a moment of stillness as Reed stood holding the dog on the top of the bridge. He regarded the sad look in the canine's eyes. There seemed to be an unnerving cognizance in them, like the animal was able to see through Reed, into his brain, and directly at his thoughts.

At his soul.

It frightened him, and when Reed noticed his own reflection staring back at him from the dog's eyes, he had to look away.

Storm clouds billowed in, darkening the scene like a theater about to start its feature presentation. Lightning forked the sky, and a sudden gust of wind came over the bridge like a powerful wave. Reed knew the sky was about to drop at any moment, and if he had any intention of following through with his idea, he couldn't waste any more time stalling.

"Don't worry," Reed told the dog, forcing a smile that suggested he was coddling—and persuading—only himself. "You're going to be okay."

Thunder boomed, louder than Reed was expecting and powerful enough to shake the structure under his feet. He jumped in reaction to it, and Reed didn't so much drop the dog as he did toss it into the air like a hot potato.

The dog flew over the edge of the bridge, clipping its backside on the metal railing before falling into the raging waters of the Hiltzik River. It hit the choppy surface with a pronounced slap.

"Shit," Reed huffed. He wasn't upset about tossing the dog—he planned to throw it over anyway—but was mostly embarrassed to be caught off guard by something so trivial.

Reed looked down and watched the current snag the dog akin to a fishhook snaring a bluegill. The river carried the animal beneath the water, under the bridge, and out of sight.

Reed removed his shirt and ran to the other side of the structure. He anticipated it would only be a few seconds before the dog would complete its pass under the bridge and reappear for him to jump in after it. His fingers found the edge of the metal railing and tightened around it. He waited.

Five seconds passed. The dog didn't resurface.

Then ten seconds passed.

Fifteen.

Twenty.

Half a minute later, and there was still no sign of the dog. Reed slapped the railing. What the hell was happening? Why wasn't the dog reappearing?

Reed looked down at the bridge, unable to see through the structure but imagining what might've happened right under his feet.

The damn thing must've gotten caught on something, Reed presumed. There must be a grate under the bridge, or a wedged log, or even an entire beaver dam down there. The dog is probably stuck and unsure how to get itself out.

"Fuck," he muttered.

Reed backtracked off the bridge, feeling the first drops of rain strike his bare shoulders as he maneuvered toward the underside of the bridge. He was irritated by the unexpected hiccup with the dog and concerned he'd probably have to redo the entire thing—if that was even possible with the rain coming down harder by the second. He pictured his phone sitting atop the bridge getting more and more soaked, and his irritation simmered into bubbling anger. Still, he swallowed his resentment and trudged across the sandbar, almost slipping on a soft patch of mud but thankfully avoiding that disaster. He rounded the corner of the structure and stepped under the bridge.

The underside of the bridge was darker than Reed was expecting—so drenched in shadows it took a moment for his eyes to adjust to the change. It was louder here, too, the sounds of the choppy water feeling amplified in a way that seemed larger than life.

The space also magnified the sound of the dog's whimpering. Reed looked out and saw the animal stuck in the middle of the river. Its entire body was submerged under the water, likely stuck on something sitting on the riverbed. The dog's small head barely broke the surface as it stretched for air. Waves slapped the dog's face as it locked eyes with Reed and cried for his help.

"Goddamnit," Reed said. Now he'd have to rescue the dog out of view of his recording phone.

So much for going viral again.

Reed removed his shoes and socks and stepped into the river. The water was cold against his ankles, and he recoiled at the sensation of the riverbed's muddy contents rising up and curling between his toes.

"I'm coming, buddy," Reed said as he took careful step after careful step.

The water crawled up Reed's legs and to his waist. The river was deeper than he had imagined, and he was surprised when the water eventually reached his shoulders.

"Almost there," he told the dog.

Reed took another step, and the heel of his foot abruptly found the sharp point of a broken beer bottle lying latent on the riverbed. The glassy dagger broke through his skin, and Reed instinctively brought his whole leg up to his chest and palmed his foot. A cloud of blood warmed his fingers.

Just a few feet ahead, the dog continued to whine.

Reed gritted his teeth. He released his hold on his injured foot and regarded the crying animal with a look of contempt. Between his recording phone being left exposed on top of the bridge, and now the open wound on his foot that was likely going to require stitches, Reed faltered at the idea of pursuing this endeavor any further.

"Sorry, buddy," Reed said to the dog and took a decisive step back. "You're just not worth all this trouble."

He made to turn back to the sandbar, inclined to leave the animal in the wild river, but he stopped. He thought maybe the pain in his foot was affecting his acuity, but as he looked back at the dog, he was surprised to see the animal slowly rising out of the water.

Reed rubbed his eyes, confident he was just momentarily delusional, but when he checked again, he was still seeing the same thing. The dog's full head appeared out of the water, followed by its neck and prosternum, and then finally by its shoulders and legs as it sat perched atop something hidden beneath the waves.

Something hidden and *rising*.

Reed looked at the dog, then at the thing underneath it as it gradually revealed itself. It had a coarse exterior, like the surface of a mountainside, and it was covered in splotches of moss and growing algae. If Reed had to guess, he might've assumed it was a massive boulder somehow ballooning to the surface of the river.

It wasn't until Reed saw the eyes that he knew it wasn't a boulder and instead the head of something he believed—up until this point—existed only in storybooks.

The eyes were red and pointy and the size of footballs, and

they sat neatly atop a stony, bulbous nose with two enlarged nostrils leaking river water.

Then there was the mouth—a black opening that took up half its face, protected by the sharp points of hundreds of rocky teeth. Water spilled out of the thing's mouth as the entirety of its head emerged from the river.

Reed stood motionless, the pain in his injured foot a sudden nonfactor to the sight of the monster's massive head staring directly at him.

The dog sat comfortably on top of it.

Reed considered his limited options—fight or flight—and didn't take long to commit to a decision.

Don't feed the trolls, he thought again.

Two giant hands of earth and stone appeared next to the monstrous face, prompting Reed to turn around and book it back to the safety of the sandbar. The face watched him as the hands steadily extended outward in opposite directions in the same manner of someone blocking traffic. Then, when a fleeing Reed had reached the ideal distance, the heavy hands swept across the surface of the water and came together in a final clapping motion, right where the influencer stood.

The hands pulverized Reed. His head exploded upward like the cap on a new tube of toothpaste being launched under pressure. A geyser of blood and brain matter painted the underside of the bridge as Reed's head rebounded on the structure, fell back into the water, and drifted away.

When the clapping echo of Reed's demise dimmed to nothing, the gore-splattered hands finally separated. They retreated back to the dog—still perched atop the gargantuan head—and offered the canine first dibs on lunch. The dog wagged its tail and set its eyes on a perfectly sized lump of meat and bone that was once Reed's forearm. The dog tiptoed onto one of the earthy palms, took the bloody chunk of Reed into its jaws, and allowed itself to be carried to the sandbar. Then the dog excitedly trekked up the riverbank—*trip trap trip trap*—before remembering to quiet its steps as it reached the bridge. It silently crossed and returned to its favorite spot to enjoy its meal.

Under the bridge, the troll gobbled up the remainder of Reed and licked its palms clean. Satisfied and with a full belly, the troll sank beneath the surface of the water where it would patiently listen for the sound of its next casualty tripping over its bridge.

THE KNOCKER-UP

It was just after four in the morning when Grace awakened to her son standing next to her bed.

"Mommy, there's a man at my window."

"Wha—*what?*" Grace sat up with a start and flicked on the bedside lamp.

"There's a man outside," the seven-year-old said. "He was tapping on the glass."

Grace sighed and rubbed the sleep from her eyes. "There can't be a man tapping on your window, Michael. Your room is on the second floor."

"He's standing down below," Michael revealed. "On the sidewalk."

"Then how is he tapping?"

"With a really big stick."

Grace was reluctant to believe him—and even more reluctant to leave the comfort of her bed. She had just exhausted herself moving everything into their historic and newly renovated townhome and wanted nothing more than some undisturbed rest.

"Come see, Mommy!" Michael insisted.

Grace threw off the covers and curiously followed her son back to his room. They approached the single hung window and looked down at the empty sidewalk below.

"I don't see anyone," Grace said. "Are you sure this wasn't a dream?"

"I saw him," Michael maintained.

Grace didn't trust her son's conviction but still mustered the energy to feign confidence in him. "Well, the man's gone now. Let's get you back to bed."

Grace tucked Michael in and sat with him until he fell asleep, which thankfully didn't take more than a few minutes. Then Grace made to leave the room, accidentally stumbling on one of the moving boxes Michael had left strewn across the floor. She'd have to remind him to put the rest of his stuff away in the morning.

———

"Mommy, the man's at my window again!"

It was the next night, just after four in the morning, and Grace felt a touch of déjà vu seeing her son standing next to her bed.

"Hurry!" Michael demanded. "Come look before he goes away!"

Before Grace could even turn on the light, her son took off.

"Michael, wait!" Doubtful of his claim but still precautious to the possibility of it being true, Grace jumped out of bed and quickly followed her son to his room. She caught up with him at his window, and together, they looked out into the darkness.

Just like the previous night, the sidewalk was empty.

"No one's outside," Grace said.

"He was *right there*," Michael asserted.

Grace let out a relieved—albeit frustrated—breath. She was sure the recent move had caused Michael some untoward stress, leading to this sudden bout of strange and vivid dreams.

"I don't see anybody," Grace said. "Come on, kiddo. You need to sleep. You start school today."

———

THE NIGHTLY INCIDENTS CONTINUED THROUGHOUT the week, and when Michael waltzed into his mother's bedroom for the fifth night in a row, Grace had had enough.

"Michael, this has to stop."

"But the man came back!" Michael swore. "He even talked to me this time!"

Grace kept her eyes half-closed and the blanket up to her chin. "Is the man still outside?"

Michael shrugged.

"Well, if he's out there, tell him to go away and to not come back."

Michael left the room, and Grace went back to sleep.

———

ON FRIDAY AND SATURDAY NIGHT, GRACE SLEPT soundly. Michael didn't come into her room, affording Grace the best two nights of sleep she'd had in months.

With plenty of rest, Grace was able to clear her mind and check her frustrations about the situation. She sat calmly with Michael for Sunday breakfast, hoping to have a talk with him about how he was coping with the move. She figured a chat about the alleged window-tapper would be the perfect jumping-off point.

"Kiddo, I noticed you didn't come into my room the last

couple nights," Grace said. "I guess that man finally left for good."

"Nope," Michael opposed as he nonchalantly chewed on a piece of toast. "He just doesn't work on the weekend."

Grace leaned in. "He doesn't *work?*"

"That's why he keeps waking me up," Michael said. "It's his job."

"What job?"

"He's a knocker-up," Michael explained. "He knocks on windows and wakes people up so they can start their day."

"Like an alarm clock?" Grace inquired.

"Don't say alarm clocks around Billy," Michael advised.

"Billy?"

"That's his name. Billy the Knocker-Up."

"And Billy doesn't like alarm clocks?"

"He *hates* them," Michael divulged. "He said he used to love waking people up so they could go to work, and everybody who worked at the factory loved him, too. Then people got alarm clocks and didn't need him anymore, and they forgot about him."

"Then why is he still waking you up?" Grace asked.

Michael swallowed. "He doesn't want to be forgotten anymore."

———

AFTER THE CONVERSATION AT BREAKFAST, GRACE was sure the knocker-up was less a recurring dream and more the ruse of a demented stranger. She imagined some cracked-out geezer roaming the streets every night, shouting off stories to anyone willing to listen—her vulnerable and newly relocated son being the only assured listener for miles.

Over the following week, Michael continued to insist on nightly visits from the stranger, and since the man was always gone by the time she was alerted, Grace concocted a plan to catch the bastard in the act and get rid of him for good.

She'd set her alarm to go off five minutes to four, allowing her enough time to wake up, walk into Michael's room, and confront the man tapping on the window. She'd ask him to stop harassing them, and—if it came to it—she'd threaten to call the police if he refused to leave, or if he decided to make the imprudent decision to ever come back.

One thing was certain: this whole knocker-up business ended tonight.

———

AT FIVE MINUTES TO FOUR, GRACE'S ALARM sounded. Groggy and disoriented, she nearly hit the snooze button out of reflex until she remembered the plan and forcibly dragged herself out of bed.

Grace slipped on a bathrobe, tiptoed to her son's room, and stood next to the window with her arms crossed.

She waited.

Grace rested her head against the wall, her tired eyes fighting to stay open. After several minutes passed without sound or movement, she began to wonder if she was just wasting her time waiting on someone who didn't exist outside of her son's imagination.

Then, at exactly four in the morning, she heard it.

Tap, tap, tap.

Grace looked at the window and saw the end of a long stick rapping against the glass.

Tap, tap, tap.

In his bed, Michael stirred at the sound, and when he opened his eyes and saw his mother standing on the opposite end of the room, he opened his mouth to say something to her.

Grace silently motioned for Michael to stay quiet and promptly yanked the window open.

"Hey!" she called out into the darkness.

Looking down, Grace followed the raised stick to its possessor below—a tall and lanky man standing on the sidewalk and cloaked in shadow. Grace couldn't see his face—the shadows of the night made it an empty cavity of blackness—but the tilt of his head suggested the man was looking back at her.

"You need to leave!" Grace shouted down. "Stop coming here and waking up my son!"

The man on the sidewalk said nothing.

"Are you hearing me?" Grace asked. "Don't tap on this window ever again!"

Still no response from the shadowy figure.

"If I catch you here one more time, I'm calling the police!"

On that note, Grace intended to slam the window shut—a perfect bookend to a perfect threat—but when she saw the man still standing in silence and looking up at her, a cold chill moved down her spine, into her feet, and froze her to the spot.

Finally, the man looked away. He rested the long stick against his shoulder like a military rifle and continued down the sidewalk.

Once he was out of sight, Grace shut the window. She moved to the door and looked back at her son, who was suddenly sitting upright in bed and regarding her with an expression of unease. His small chest swelled and deflated with heavy, unnerved breaths.

"You shouldn't have done that," Michael said in a flat voice. Then he jumped out of bed and ran to the window, his worry turning to panic when he noticed the empty sidewalk below. *"You shouldn't have done that!"*

Michael swiftly opened the window. He stuck his head

out of the opening, and for a split second, Grace thought her son was actually going to jump.

"Michael!" Grace shrieked and ran over to him.

"SHE DIDN'T MEAN IT!" Michael screamed into the darkness. "PLEASE—SHE DIDN'T MEAN IT!"

Grace grabbed her son by the back of his pajamas and pulled him inside.

Michael struggled against her, blindly intent on calling out to the man outside.

"Stop it, Michael!" Grace pleaded, tugging her son away with one arm and closing the window with the other. Then she turned him around and looked into his eyes. "What has gotten into you?!"

Michael's eyes darted between his mother and the window, but he said nothing.

"Michael?" Grace said, her voice softer this time.

Her son put his chin to his chest and started to cry.

Grace, taken aback and unsure what to do, pulled Michael close to her and wrapped her arms around him. She couldn't pinpoint her son's feelings and wondered why he was so upset.

Was Michael worried the man would never come back?

Was he worried that he *would?*

"It's okay, kiddo," Grace soothed, even though she was beginning to feel the early pings of worry herself. "It's okay…"

———

THE NEXT DAY, GRACE RECEIVED A CALL FROM THE school. Michael wasn't feeling well.

"Does he have a fever?" Grace asked the school nurse.

"No fever," the nurse replied. "It could be something he ate, or a stomach bug. He's just complaining that his tummy feels upset."

Grace figured it had something to do with the prior

night's events and didn't ask any additional questions. She picked up Michael from school and brought him home, having him rest on the couch so she could closely monitor him throughout the day.

Michael gratefully didn't show any obvious signs of sickness while he was home, but he also didn't sleep. Instead of acting sick, he appeared anxious—*afraid*, even.

At nightfall, Grace cooked something light for dinner, managing to sneak some drowsy over-the-counter medicine into Michael's portion to help him catch some Z's.

"Mommy," Michael said just before falling asleep, "if Billy comes back tonight, will you go to the window? Will you make sure he sees you?"

Grace knew it was the man outside who had planted a seed of worry in Michael, and this made her blood boil. She hated the notion of some stranger making her son uneasy enough to feel physically ill.

I *dare* that man to come back here, she thought.

"I promise, kiddo."

Within half an hour, Michael was snoring. Grace thought about carrying him up the stairs to his bed, but since he was sleeping so soundly—and since he seemed wary of his own room—she opted against it.

He'll be better down here, she told herself.

———

Grace bolted awake to the shrill sound of her alarm clock. She punched the device in a panic, almost knocking it to the floor. She struck it a second time, and the alarm silenced.

Regaining some calm, Grace checked the clock. Five minutes to four. She silently cursed herself for accidentally setting the alarm to reoccur daily.

No matter. Now that she was awake, she could take the opportunity to check on Michael in the living room.

Grace was halfway down the steps when she heard something on the second floor, coming from Michael's bedroom.

Tap, tap, tap.

The man was back.

Grace marched up the steps in a fury, consumed by rage and ready to give the man a piece of her mind.

She stormed into Michael's room and crossed through the darkness. She was almost at the window when her foot jammed into one of the moving boxes still occupying the floor. She never did remind Michael to put his stuff away. Pain surged through Grace's toes as she shrieked and fell forward, her head striking the wall and splitting her cheek just before she hit the floor.

Grace groaned. She collected herself and struggled to her feet, blindly feeling for the nearest piece of furniture to support her weight and assist in her standing.

Tap, tap, tap.

Fuck off! Grace's mind screamed as she finally stood tall. The throbbing in her toes quickly moved up her leg, through her abdomen, and into her head, where it exploded in her right cheek like a peony firework. She touched her face, and her fingertips came back with the wetness of blood.

Grace pushed through the pain, opened the window, and yelled out into the night.

"I told you to stay away from here!" she cried. *"I'm calling the police!"*

Grace looked down, and her enraged face softened.

The sidewalk was empty.

The man wasn't there.

Grace looked around, swallowing the lump that had formed in her throat. She checked the sidewalk again, then a third time just to be sure, but her eyes weren't misleading her. The man simply wasn't outside.

She timidly closed the window and turned for the bathroom to clean the wound on her cheek—a lovely superficial cut that promised a good bruise later. Then, once she had cleaned herself up, Grace returned to her initial task of checking on her son downstairs.

Michael was still asleep on the couch when Grace took a seat by his feet. He steadily stirred awake, and when he saw his mother sitting next to him, he swiftly bolted upright, his face etched with an astute awareness.

"Did Billy come back?!" he demanded.

Grace rested her hand on Michael's shoulder to soothe him. "Don't worry, kiddo. Mommy's here."

"Did he come back?!" Michael repeated. "Did Billy see you?!"

"He came back," Grace said. "I went to the window to speak to him, but he was already gone by the time I got there. I'm going to the police station in the morning to file a report. I'm sorry this keeps happening, but this will all be over soon."

She thought Michael would find comfort in her words, but the opposite was true. His wide, fearful eyes grew even wider.

"You promised," Michael whispered. "You promised Billy would see you."

Grace couldn't understand her son's concern. "Michael, what's going on?"

"If you don't go to the window when Billy knocks, he'll be angry. He'll think you've forgotten him like everybody else. Like the people at the factory. Like the people who lived here before us."

Grace looked at her son with a similar expression of astute awareness. She was going to ask Michael if he knew what happened to those factory workers, or the people who previously lived in their townhome—*a sinking feeling in her gut told her she already knew*—but her attention was diverted by the sound of something small and mechanical being smashed upstairs.

"What the hell was that?" Grace asked.

"It's Billy," Michael said.

Another sound emerged from the second floor, and Grace and Michael whipped their heads in time to see a shattered wind-up alarm clock plummet to the bottom of the stairs.

"Billy didn't see you at the window," Michael continued. "He thinks you've forgotten him. Now he's inside, and he wants to make everyone forget *you*."

A dark shadow fell over the top of the landing. Its bearer held a long, crude stick in its hand—encrusted with blood—and used it to strike each step as it came down the stairs.

Tap.

Tap.

Tap.

Mercy at the End of Her Life

"What's Mercy doing now?" Henry Conole grumbled. He parked his Prius against the curb of 137 Jasper Lane and looked at the neo-eclectic house crawling with landscapers.

Henry's wife, Laura, didn't turn her head from the passenger seat. The couple had just returned from the grocery store, itself an exhausting experience, and Laura wanted nothing more than to unload the bags and relax on the couch. Listening to her husband of thirty years play his almighty role as president of the Homeowner's Association—a position she hated and wished he'd never acquired ten years ago—was not high on her list of tasks for the day.

"Are those fence posts?" Henry probed, his voice carrying anger and disbelief. "Is she actually having a fence built around her front yard?"

Laura finally glanced up. "Looks like a white picket fence."

"She's lost her mind," Henry growled.

"It's cute," Laura remarked.

"It's not allowed!"

Henry shut off the engine and unclicked his seatbelt.

"Henry, please—" Laura started, but her husband had already opened the door and left the vehicle to exchange words with the homeowner. Laura knew it'd be at least fifteen minutes before Henry returned, and another fifteen minutes of him caviling in the parked Prius before they'd finally head for home and unload the groceries.

There goes the milk, she thought.

———

AT BEDTIME, LAURA LOOKED FORWARD TO READING the latest smutty paperback she had impulsively grabbed from the checkout rack earlier in the day. She crawled into bed and opened her book when Henry barged into the room with a stack of papers. Unsurprising to Laura, he was still blathering on about the obstinate woman at 137 Jasper Lane.

"Mercy thinks she can do whatever she wants, whenever she wants," Henry sneered. "She's about to find out what happens to people who slam doors in my face."

Laura had heard all of this earlier—once when Henry first returned to the vehicle, then again at dinner. She preferred not to pay any mind to the matter, but when she permitted herself to think about it, Laura understood Mercy's reaction to Henry's reprimanding. Any rational person would close the door in the face of someone yelling at them on their own property.

Laura didn't vocalize these thoughts to her husband, though. She was smarter than that.

"Look at this," Henry continued and tossed the stack of printed spreadsheets onto the bed. "I'm tracking everything she does. Every interaction I've had with her. Every unapproved change she's made to her house. Pretty soon, her HOA fees are going to be ten times her mortgage. Then we can put a lien on her house and get her out of this neighborhood for good."

Laura lowered her book and glanced at the detailed paperwork. She knew Henry had worked on it all evening, and she conceived his meticulous obsession being valid—even impressive—to someone like-minded to him.

To Laura, it was just time-consuming, unimportant, and sad.

"I don't know what to say," Laura said. And she didn't.

Henry regarded the papers with pride while Laura regarded her husband like he was a total stranger. What had happened to the level-headed man she'd known most of her life? The man who used to buy her flowers and chocolates once a month? The man whose only obsessions were fixing old cars and collecting rare coins? Her other half who was supposed to know what she was thinking and how she was feeling without the necessity for any words at all?

He's gone, she accepted.

Laura had always feared she'd lose Henry to the appeal of another woman.

She never imagined losing him to the seduction of power.

Henry retrieved the papers from the bed and made to leave the room.

"Did Mercy say why she's having so many changes done to her home?" Laura asked, finally able to form a response.

"No," Henry said without turning around, "and I don't care."

They differed once again because, unlike her husband, Laura did.

———

THE FOLLOWING WEEK, AND THE DAY BEFORE schools would release for summer break, Henry typed up a letter about a neighborhood party at the community swim-ming pool and arranged for fliers to be delivered to each house. When he told his wife he'd be gone for an hour or so as he passed out the fliers, Laura stepped up and volunteered to distribute them herself.

"Don't give one to Mercy," Henry advised. "She's not up to date on her fees."

Laura said nothing but nodded in understanding.

At first, it felt great getting out of the house and walking around the neighborhood, but as her step count increased, so did the pain in her feet and knees. Laura was sixty-one, and while she wasn't in bad shape, she was gallingly starting to feel her age. A walk that was once relaxing and undemanding was now unexpectedly arduous.

Still, Laura's excitement to be out of the house and away from Henry was worth the momentary hardship.

When Laura got to the mailbox for 137 Jasper Lane, she stopped and reflected.

In spite of her husband's decree that Mercy shouldn't receive a flier, Laura had made up her own mind that she was going to deliver one anyway. But first, Laura wanted to have a face-to-face conversation with Mercy. In the eight years since Mercy first moved to the neighborhood, the two women had only been in close proximity to each other a few times—and exchanged the briefest of small talk once. Laura thought it would be nice to have a civil conversation with Mercy and explain to her how Henry's zeal was not a sentiment she shared.

With an encouraging breath, Laura traipsed up the driveway and rang the doorbell.

After a moment, the door opened, and Laura was surprised to be greeted by a woman other than Mercy—a short, spritely gal she hadn't seen before. She appeared to be in her late twenties and had long, chestnut hair pulled back into a messy ponytail. Laura studied the woman's face, thinking she might find a hint of Mercy's likeness in her features, giving her the clearance to presume the stranger was a visiting relative. But Laura saw no likeness to Mercy at all. So who *was* this woman?

"Can I help you?" the woman asked.

"Hello," Laura said amicably. "My name is Laura. I live in the blue house on Windward. I'm sorry to bother you, but is Mercy home?"

"She is, but she can't come to the door right now," the woman said. "Mercy had to be taken to the hospital last night and just got home a few hours ago. She's resting in bed now. I'm her home health nurse, Nina."

The two exchanged an awkward handshake.

"I'm so sorry," Laura said, and she meant it. Laura knew Mercy was ten years younger and in fantastic shape, and she couldn't fathom why a person so outwardly healthy would have to be admitted to the hospital so suddenly—or why she would require a home health nurse. "I was just dropping off a flier and thought I'd say hello. Was Mercy in an accident? I wasn't aware anything had happened."

"No accident," Nina replied. "Mercy's real sick. She has throat cancer. Doctors discovered it in March and only gave her a few months to—" She stopped in fear of oversharing with a total stranger. "Anyway, I'll be here on and off to check in with Mercy and assist, so if you see a blue Honda in the driveway, that's me."

Laura managed a sympathetic frown when Nina gave her a curious look of cognizance.

"Wait a minute. You said your name's Laura?"

"Yes."

"Laura Conole?"

Her eyes widened. "That's right."

Nina retreated from the open door and disappeared into

the house. After a moment, she returned carrying a spiral notebook that had been folded open to a page with a handwritten list. She gestured for Laura to look at it.

"What's this?" Laura asked.

"Mercy's bucket list," Nina said. "Take a look."

Laura eyed the paper and graceful penmanship. There were twelve individual objectives Mercy had written down that she hoped to accomplish before she passed, and all but three of them had already been crossed off.

The tasks that remained unchecked were:

> *paint my front door red*
> *ride in the back of a cop car*
> *see Laura Conole smile*

Laura did a double-take and read the last task again. Was that really her own name staring back at her from the page?

Nina looked at Laura with an equally quizzical look. "Mercy can't speak anymore, so I can't ask her why she wrote that last one," Nina said. "I doubt she would tell me if she could. Do *you* know why she wrote it, Mrs. Conole?"

Laura didn't respond because—no.

She didn't have a clue.

LAURA TRIED TO SLEEP BUT COULDN'T WITH Henry's snoring prevailing over the white noise machine sitting on the nightstand.

She also couldn't stop thinking about Mercy's bucket list.

The list explained so much to Laura. It enlightened her as to why Mercy had done so many updates to her home in such a short period of time—like the white picket fence she had built last week. It rationalized why Mercy wasn't worried about the penalties that would befall her for not getting approval from the HOA. She simply wouldn't be around long enough to be affected by the consequences.

Laura thought about the unfinished tasks on Mercy's list.

paint my front door red

Henry will love that, she thought sarcastically.

ride in the back of a cop car

Henry will love that even more. No sarcasm.

see Laura Conole smile

That one puzzled her.

Why would Mercy want to see me smile? Laura wondered. *Does Mercy think I have "resting bitch face," or whatever the kids are calling it? Does she think I'm incapable of smiling, or that I'm unapproachable? Maybe she's implying she wants me to be happy. Does she know that I'm not? How long has it been since I last smiled, anyway?*

These thoughts churned and repeated, circling about her mind as if caught in a funnel.

Laura looked at her sleeping husband. She wondered if she should share this new information with him—wondered if the knowledge of Mercy's situation would change his excessive fervency against her. Surely if he knew the reason behind Mercy's motivations, he'd be a little more sympathetic and back off with his overbearing tyranny. Henry was stubborn, but he wasn't *that* heartless—was he?

Laura was certain telling him the truth would bring a welcome change.

She'd share the news with him first thing in the morning.

Laura closed her eyes and let the soothing sound of the white noise machine—and Henry's loathsome snoring—put her to sleep.

———

LAURA AWOKE THE NEXT MORNING TO AN EMPTY bed. She looked out the bedroom window, curious to see the Prius missing from the driveway. Retrieving her phone, she checked her notifications and found a text from Henry: *Going to the store. Be back soon.*

She sighed, realizing she'd have to wait a little longer to tell Henry the news about Mercy.

Laura went downstairs and made a cup of coffee. She sat on a barstool at the kitchen island, where Henry's spreadsheets had already claimed dominion over the granite surface. With a huff, she brushed the papers away, clearing a spot to rest her mug. She paused when something on one of the spreadsheets caught her attention.

Picking up the paper, Laura's eyes zeroed in on one of Henry's notations:

———

April 11: Observed resident of 137 Jasper Lane painting the exterior shutters a new color. Advised homeowner it was against policy to do this without HOA approval. Resident informed me she was "dying of cancer anyway" and to "fuck off."

———

At first, reading Mercy's response to the warning made Laura want to snicker, but as the sudden realizations about Henry became apparent, her jaw went slack and hung open with surprise and disgust.

Henry had lied to her.

He knew about Mercy's condition this whole time.

And he didn't care.

The paper fell from her grasp and drifted back to the counter like an autumnal leaf.

Laura's deepest fear had proven true.

Her husband really was that heartless.

———

LAURA DIDN'T WANT TO GO TO THE NEIGHBORHOOD pool party, and Henry's insistence for her to attend only made her more disposed to stay home.

"I don't feel like going," she told Henry from the bed, but what she really meant was, *I don't want to be anywhere near you.*

Since discovering the inconvenient truth about her husband a few weeks ago, Laura had made every effort to avoid him—and limit his access to her. She stayed up all night and slept during the day, revolted by the thought of sharing a bed with him. She cooked her own meals, deliberately preparing dishes she knew Henry hated just so she could eat alone. She closed and locked the bathroom door, even if she was only using the space to brush her teeth, wash her hands, or to just sit on the closed toilet seat and play on her phone.

She didn't know how long the avoidance could go on, but until she could figure out how to process this unbecoming revelation about the man she thought she knew, it was the only thing she could reason to do.

"I *really* want you at the pool party," Henry stressed from the bedroom doorway. "People will expect you to be there."

"Why should I care what other people think?" she asked him. For a moment, Laura felt a ping of Mercy's influence in the room with them, and it warmed her broken heart.

"You should care what *I* think," he said.

She didn't—and never would again.

"Be ready in thirty minutes." He left the room, depriving her the chance to argue.

Laura got dressed.

Ultimately, the party at the community pool wasn't as bad as Laura had imagined it would be. With all her neighbors in attendance, it gave her the chance to mingle and lose herself in the shuffle—*away* from Henry, which she wanted most of all.

As Laura circled the crowd, she discovered there was one person still unaccounted for.

Laura recalled her interaction with Mercy's home health nurse, and she realized she had been so sidetracked by their talk that she had never actually handed over a copy of the flier. Mercy likely didn't even know there was a party. Laura believed that, even if she wasn't well enough to attend, Mercy still merited the invite. She deserved to know she hadn't been forgotten.

Feeling guilty, Laura excused herself from conversation and skirted for the nearest exit. She didn't want to walk to 137 Jasper Lane, knowing the pain in her joints and muscles was imminent if she went by foot, but she also didn't want Henry badgering her with questions if she asked for the keys to drive there. The forthcoming pain from walking was a welcomed amnesty from Henry possibly denying her request and feasibly holding any more authority over her than he already had.

Laura checked the party for Henry, wanting to sneak away without notice.

She didn't see him.

Perfect, her mind breathed in relief. *If I can't see him, he can't see me leave.*

Laura quietly exited, confident with her decision and eager to see Mercy. It had been so long since her first attempt to talk to her. In spite of the two almost never communicating directly, Laura felt an unspoken bond with the woman—a bond that was, for whatever reason, becoming stronger and more tangible by the day. Maybe it was Mercy's unwavering pushback to authority, which Laura admired. Maybe it was the way Mercy had told Henry off before losing her ability to speak—something Laura wished she was brave enough to do with the voice she still had. Maybe it was the fact that they were two women trapped in unpleasant realities where death seemed to be the only absolution.

Whatever it was, Laura felt drawn to Mercy's magnetic pull, and she willingly surrendered to it as she finally reached Jasper Lane. She approached the house with the white picket fence and the numbers 1-3-7 on its mailbox.

Laura stopped.

Was that Henry's Prius parked across the street?

———

"I *REALLY* WANT YOU AT THE POOL PARTY," HENRY told his wife. "People will expect you to be there."

That wasn't entirely true, but he couldn't tell Laura the real reason he wanted her at the party—not even if she was on his side, which she wasn't. Her behavior over the last several weeks had made that perfectly evident: ignoring Henry, no longer cooking his meals, and only sleeping in the bed when he wasn't in it. Laura had completely changed in a way that excluded him from her life, and it all seemed to have started the day she passed out fliers around the neighborhood.

He couldn't be sure, but Henry believed Mercy was

somehow responsible for Laura's mutiny. He felt it in his gut, and with that feeling came boundless questions. Had the two women interacted and become friends without him knowing? Were numbers exchanged between them? Did they text each other every day? That had to be why Laura was locking herself in the bathroom all the time. Where else would Laura have learned such wayward behavior?

The thought of losing Laura to the influence of someone like Mercy made Henry rage. He hated Mercy—hated her resistance to order; hated her constant opposition; hated how she humiliated him by going against his agency. The added suspicion that Mercy was adversely impacting his wife was just fuel to a fire he had lit long ago.

Henry knew what he had to do, and he'd been planning it since the day that bitch slammed her door in his face.

The pool party was the first step—and the perfect diversion for him to pull everything off.

He just needed Laura to be in attendance, too.

In the bedroom, the married couple exchanged more quarreling words before Henry ended the conversation with a simple and inarguable, "Be ready in thirty minutes."

That took care of that.

Half an hour later, Henry and Laura showed up at the community pool in the Prius, went their separate ways at the party, and individually greeted fellow neighbors.

Henry navigated the crowd for about ten minutes, socializing with his peers and making sure everyone noticed him in attendance. Then, when he broke away from the group, he silently slunk away from the venue and back to the parking lot.

He thought about walking to Mercy's house to carry out his plan, but time was a factor, and walking would eat up too much of it he didn't have. He elected to drive because it was faster, and he doubted anyone would see or hear the Prius as it pulled away.

Thank goodness for hybrid vehicles, he thought.

As the Prius silently covered the empty neighborhood, Henry blindly reached into the backseat and retrieved a ball-peen hammer from the floorboard. He'd recently purchased it from a hardware store several towns over (paid in cash) and stashed it there for this very occasion. Now it sat tightly in his fist as he drove one-handed and reflected on his plan.

During one of his routine neighborhood watch drives, Henry noticed a sixteen-foot extension ladder resting against the side of Mercy's house. It was the same ladder he caught Mercy standing on months ago when she painted her window shutters without approval.

It was seeing this ladder that put the better part of Henry's plan into motion.

If Henry could just lure Mercy outside and toward the ladder, it wouldn't take more than a single hammer blow to the head to bring her down. He'd leave her body there and knock the ladder over with his foot, letting it fall next to her, staging an accident. Then he'd immediately return to the party, where people would assume—and attest—he had been circulating the entire time.

He'd take care of the hammer later.

As president of the HOA, police would likely question him about Mercy's death, and he'd show them all his documentation of Mercy completing various unauthorized projects around her home: installing new light fixtures, building fences, painting shutters. He'd tell the officers how he advised against each project, and how it was only a matter of time before poor Mercy electrocuted herself, cut her hand in a miter saw, or—as it turned out—fell off a ladder.

Henry's heart rate reached a personal record as feelings of thrill and accomplishment stirred within him. He knew Mercy was dying and would probably go belly-up any day now, and anyone else in his position would likely just let her pass on her own.

Not Henry.

Mercy was dying, but the woman was simultaneously pulling Laura away from him. How much longer did she need on this earth to accomplish that, and how much time was Henry supposed to allow to go by while she succeeded in taking away what belonged to him?

Mercy needed to die sooner rather than later, he thought.

She *deserved* to die.

Why delay the inevitable?

The Prius pulled up to 137 Jasper Lane, and for a moment, Henry's fast-beating heart completely stopped.

Mercy was already outside.

The frail woman stood on her front porch, paintbrush in hand and an open gallon of red paint at her feet. The crimson-speckled lid sat upside down on a plastic tarp between the paint can and the flat head screwdriver she had used to pry it off.

Mercy was painting her front door red.

No, Henry thought. This threw everything off. Mercy was already out of the house, and that was okay. She was tackling another unauthorized home renovation project, and that was somehow okay, too—but the project in question couldn't be Mercy *painting her front door*. She wouldn't need an extension ladder for that. How was Henry supposed to stage an accident with a ladder if Mercy was performing a task that went against the idea?

Just one more way for her to spite me, he thought.

Henry needed to restrategize—and fast.

He pitched the hammer into the passenger seat and parked the Prius against the curb opposite Mercy's house. He drummed his fingers against the steering wheel and mentally thumbed through the Rolodex of ideas in his head—elaborate plots that were far too grandiose for last-minute improvisation.

It just needs to look like an accident, Henry reminded himself.

A silly little accident.

Mercy continued painting, her back to Henry, oblivious to his presence.

Henry knew he was wasting precious time and needed to figure out a new plan before Mercy turned around and spotted him—and before the attendees at the party noticed his absence.

Henry's gaze drifted to the red can of paint sitting directly behind Mercy.

Bingo.

He could see it now—Mercy applying a fresh coat of paint to the door; Mercy stepping back to admire her handiwork; forgetting the can of paint sitting behind her; tripping over it; whacking her head on one of the front-step pillars; falling to the ground and bleeding out from the back of her skull.

A silly little accident, Officer.

With renewed purpose, Henry grinned and picked up the hammer. He opened the driver's door and quietly emerged from the vehicle, nearly closing the door out of habit before acknowledging the unnecessary noise it would generate. He didn't want to alert Mercy to his approach, so he grabbed at the swinging door and kept it open. Then, with a relieved breath, he crept across the street, hammer at his side, the hard striking face of the instrument brushing against his khaki shorts. He cleared the tarmac, stepped over the curb, and began his way across the grassy front lawn.

He hadn't crossed but half the yard when Mercy abruptly stopped painting and opened the front door. At first, it looked like she had only opened the door to paint the edges. Then Mercy haphazardly tossed the paintbrush onto the plastic tarp and disappeared into the house. The door shut behind her.

Henry hesitated, unsure if he should continue forward. Was Mercy just going inside the house to grab something? Get a drink? Use the restroom? Or had she seen him wielding the hammer—maybe in one of the window reflections—and quietly removed herself from the approaching danger without drawing attention to knowing he was there?

No. There was no way Mercy saw him coming. He'd bet his life on it.

She'd be back.

Henry advanced on the front porch and stepped up to the door. He considered entering the home to follow after Mercy, his tight timetable hanging over him like a specter, but he quickly resolved against the thought. No one knew a house better than the person living in it, and Mercy—sick or not— could easily find a way to get the upper hand of him if he stepped into her territory. And even *if* Henry successfully dispatched Mercy on her own turf, the timetable didn't allow for clean-up in a home he was never meant to enter—and it certainly didn't allow staging the body on the front porch where it should've been in the first place.

It was best to stay outside and wait for Mercy to return.

He'd be ready for her.

Hands trembling, Henry gripped the handle of the hammer like a felling ax and brought it over his head, keen to strike at the first sign of movement. The excitement of it all was overwhelming, and for almost a minute, Henry could hear only his heartbeat in his ears, the rapid *ba-dum, ba-dum* drowning out the world around him. It wasn't until he exhaled a long-held breath that he discerned a new sound arising.

Footsteps.

Approaching footsteps.

Mercy was already coming back.

Henry gripped the raised hammer a little tighter, practically salivating with anticipation. His tongue flicked across his thin lips. His brow furrowed, and his forehead creased into horizontal slits like closed window blinds steadily turning open.

Let's see you slam the door in my face this time, bitch.

He primed himself for victory when a deep pain—palpable, sudden, and bewildering—swelled in the base of his spine. It was a pain so intense he involuntarily released his hold on the raised hammer. The instrument fell from Henry's grip and struck him on the top of his balding head. It bounced off his skull and clattered to the porch.

Dazed, Henry glanced back. What he saw brought the insight that the approaching footsteps he'd heard hadn't come from inside the house, but instead behind him.

Henry's wife stood in back of him, her outstretched hand gripping the handle of the flat head screwdriver she had buried into his backbone. The tail of Henry's tucked-in shirt bloomed the color of ripe cherries as blood pulsed and collected there. Then, when there was nowhere left for the blood to go, it seeped through the cotton and spilled over the waistband of his shorts like the foam of a cauldron's brew. Dots of red splashed the tarp in thick, rhythmic drops.

Henry and Laura exchanged looks with a passing of not only time but crude indulgence. Laura pulled back on the screwdriver, releasing it from her husband's spine. Henry opened his mouth to say something, but she robbed him of the opportunity by sticking him again, upward and into his throat, the steel shank disappearing all the way into his neck. Henry wheezed in surprise as a bubble of blood burst from his lips.

Laura removed the tool from Henry's neck and made to

skewer him again. She faltered and dropped the screwdriver when the front door opened, and Mercy stepped through the threshold.

Henry spun in a dizzying circle, blood projecting from his exposed throat like the spray of a yard sprinkler. It misted the vacant look on Mercy's face and painted a second coat of red onto the door.

Drunk on remarkable pain, Henry teetered between the two women before collapsing to his knees. He swayed like a flower stalk and then tumbled forward, his face hitting the tarped concrete and shattering the bridge of his nose. Blood pooled out from under him, and for an instant, it was the only movement in a picture otherwise frozen in time.

Laura and Mercy regarded each other, the air as heavy as their silence. It was the first time in years Laura had seen Mercy this close in person, and seeing her in such upsetting condition made Laura feel like she was meeting her for the first time. Gone was the vibrant, energetic soul Laura had admired from afar, and in her place was a pale, gaunt skeleton devoid of hair, color, and life—an empty shell of the woman Mercy once was. There was a large, blood-spackled bandage hugging her neck, and it upset Laura even more than the mortal wound on her own husband's throat.

Looking away from the bandage, Laura glanced down, her gaze falling upon the bloodied screwdriver.

Mercy followed Laura's stare, bending down and picking up the tool for herself.

Laura took a cautious step back, unsure if Mercy was going to use the screwdriver against her in an act of self-defense.

The fragile figure that was Mercy stepped forward. With her free hand, she delicately reached up to Laura's face, finding the single speck of blood sitting atop her cheek like a forgotten tear. Mercy softly wiped it away with her thumb, cleaning the final piece of Henry not only from Laura's body, but her life.

On the street, a blue Honda turned the corner and advanced to 137 Jasper Lane. It pulled into the driveway, and a hysterical Nina emerged from the vehicle, arms raised and palms out in a pleading gesture of armistice. "Mercy, please—stop!"

As the home health nurse drew nearer, Mercy pantomimed to Laura with a flick of the eyes and an upward nod—*go*.

Laura's eyes welled with tears. She knew what Mercy was suggesting—what she was *gifting* her—and couldn't accept it.

Go, Mercy gestured again. Her blank expression softened with a smile.

Then, for the first time in a long time, Laura smiled, too.

A gift returned.

Laura backed away from a dying Mercy, away from Henry's motionless corpse, away from the veil of death and toward the unknown and hopeful future of her life.

"Mercy, what have you done?!" the home health nurse cried. She brushed past Laura, one hand reaching for the screwdriver in Mercy's possession, the other fumbling with her phone to call for help.

Laura backpedaled across the lawn. She came to the street and looked at Henry's Prius still sitting against the curb, the driver's door open, keys on the seat. With a smile on her face, Laura glided past the vehicle, weightless, her bones and muscles insisting they wouldn't betray her with the relief of a burden removed.

She kept on walking.

As the distant speck of Laura slipped over the horizon, Mercy calmly took a seat on the front step of her porch. Behind her, a distraught Nina paced with terror and stuttered into the phone, but Mercy ignored the commotion and calmly closed her eyes. She listened intently for the sound of approaching sirens.

Mercy, at the end of her life, listened for the sound of her final wish about to come true.

The Thing That Wasn't

It was ten o'clock on a Saturday night, and Heather expected the kids to be fast asleep by the time she pulled into the neighborhood. The headlights of her Buick bathed the front of the colonial house, and for a split second, Heather caught a glimpse of two eager faces in one of the upstairs windows. The sneaky little brats were staying up on purpose.

Heather grabbed her purse, got out of the car, acknowledged the parents, and exchanged the usual rhetoric with them until they quietly snuck into the garage and activated the main door with a deafening *KRRRR-EEEEE*. Then, when she was sure the parents were gone, Heather turned on some lights and called for the children to meet her downstairs.

Ethan was the first to appear, no doubt because of his irrepressible bounciness that came with the territory of being five years old. He skidded into the living room in his Disney-themed pajamas and caught himself on the wall. Then he went back to the foot of the stairs to do the same thing again. He tried this act of theatricality five or six more times before finally losing his breath and took a seat on the couch where Heather was waiting.

"Where's your sister?" Heather asked.

"Right there," Ethan said and pointed.

Courtenay, a sly fourth grader, was already sitting at the opposite end of the room, her blue eyes glowing with enthusiasm. Her blonde hair hung over her rosy cheeks until she brushed it away and bared her teeth in a flashy smile. "What did you bring for us tonight, Miss Heather?"

Shaken by the child's abrupt presence, Heather laughed nervously and sighed. "You guys are going to be disappointed," she began, trying to find the right tone with her voice. It must have been the wrong tone because, before Heather could console him, Ethan threw himself into the couch pillows and cried to the heavens.

"You're not going to be our babysitter anymore!" he wailed.

"No!" Heather immediately refuted, tousling Ethan's hair. "That's not it. I'm still going to be your babysitter. Don't worry."

Ethan wiped his eyes and sniffed. "You are?"

"Yes," Heather assured him, laughing at Ethan's quick change of the doldrums. "I'm going to be your babysitter for a long time. But tonight, there's something else I need to talk to you about." She sighed. "I need a huge favor from you guys."

Courtenay leaned forward. It was always in her nature to offer her services to someone she highly esteemed, which meant anyone old enough to run their own life, such as Miss Heather, who was eighteen and in her first year of college.

"What's the favor?" she asked with an overjoyed smile.

"Well, I really need you guys to go to bed—right now." This time, Heather's voice found the perfect balance between compassion and supremacy.

"Bed?" Ethan said.

"Yes. It's after ten o'clock, and you guys really shouldn't stay up this late. You never have before."

"But it's Saturday," Courtenay argued.

"And I'm the boss," Heather overruled.

"Why do we have to go to bed so early?" Ethan questioned.

Once again, Heather sighed. She didn't want the conversation to end up here, mostly because she knew a lack of an explanation would never put an end to this discussion. And the last thing she wanted during this babysitting cakewalk was one simple inquiry repeated a thousand times. That was a headache she couldn't handle.

"I'm going to watch a movie," Heather informed.

"What kind of movie?" Ethan asked.

"It's not for kids," Heather replied, choosing her words carefully. "It's more of a grownup movie."

"But what kind of movie is it?" Courtenay reiterated, dissatisfied with that last answer.

"It's—well—it's a scary movie," Heather breathed.

"Is it *really* scary?" Ethan wondered.

"I'm not scared of anything," Courtenay said matter-of-factly.

"It doesn't matter," Heather stated, her voice once again picking up an authoritative tone. "You guys aren't grown up enough to watch this movie."

"Yes-huh!" Courtenay openly disagreed, standing up. "I'm the bravest girl in my whole class! I'm not scared of anything!"

"Have you ever watched a scary movie before?" Heather cross-examined.

"Well, I've seen—you know—there was this one—I don't know if it counts—I mean—it wasn't exactly *scary*," Courtenay remarked, stumbling over her words. "Everyone in my class was really scared when my teacher showed it, but not me!"

"They showed it in your school?"

"Yep."

"Your teacher brought it?"

"Uh-huh."

"So you've never seen a *real* scary movie."

"I don't know," Courtenay declared. "But I wouldn't know if a movie was scary or not unless I watched it for myself."

Heather, almost convinced, licked her lips. Ethan was cuddled next to her arm, resting his cheek against her shoulder. A part of Heather didn't want Ethan to hear any of this, but she knew pressuring him to go upstairs to his bed—alone —would only put him in hysterics, especially after all this talk about scary things actually existing in his perfect, naïve world.

"Alright," Heather huffed, gently getting up from the couch so Ethan wouldn't fall flat on his face. She grabbed her purse and walked to the front entryway. "Follow me upstairs."

"Me too?" Ethan asked innocently, biting his thumb.

Heather thought for a moment, wishing he would voluntarily go to bed so she wouldn't have to force him, which she knew would never happen. The more she thought about it, the more she convinced herself this was probably the most exciting thing this kid had been through all day, and even if Ethan had to fight the Sandman with his bare hands to be here, he wasn't going to miss it.

"Alright," Heather huffed again. "Both of you. Let's go."

Together, the three marched up the steps to the top of the landing and, one after the other, walked into the master bedroom. Heather shut the door.

"Why are we in Mom and Dad's room?" Courtenay asked, confused.

"We're not supposed to be in here!" Ethan panicked.

"It's okay," Heather reassured them, turning on the bedside lamp. "You're not going to get in trouble. I promise."

"What are we doing in here?" Courtenay asked again.

"I'm going to test you," Heather revealed, "to see if you're really old enough to watch a scary movie like you say you are."

"How are you going to do that?" Courtenay inquired.

"Well," Heather began, "when I was about your age, my parents would go to the movies every weekend and leave me at home with a babysitter. I begged them to take me, too, but they said the films they saw would give me nightmares. They said I wasn't *mature* enough to understand it was all just make-believe."

Heather advanced to the walk-in closet and opened the door.

Curious, Courtenay stepped forward. Ethan nervously followed her.

"Eventually," Heather continued, "I nagged my parents to the breaking point. They caved and made a deal with me. They said if I could stay in their closet by myself—in the dark —for five minutes, I could go with them to the next movie."

"That doesn't sound so bad," Courtenay shrugged.

"Did you do it?" Ethan asked.

"I only made it for three minutes," Heather replied. "I don't remember why, but I got scared and made them open the door. But now that I'm older, I know there's nothing to be afraid of. And if you're as mature as you say you are, you'll be able to stay in the closet for five minutes like my parents made me."

"In the dark?" Courtenay asked.

"In the dark."

Courtenay ran a hand through her blonde hair. Her bright blue eyes contemplated between the bedroom door and the open closet, trying to choose between the two. She wasn't tired, not the slightest bit, but a certain trepidation hung over her back, pulling her weight down, causing her shoulders to slouch and her knees to buckle. Slowly, her trepidation turned to motivation, and her motivation turned to conviction.

"Just five minutes?" she asked.

"Just five minutes."

"Okay. If I can stay in the closet—in the dark—for five minutes, I can watch the movie. Deal?" Courtenay extended her hand.

Heather shook it and smiled. "Deal."

"Courtenay, don't!" Ethan cried, encasing her with his arms, as if anticipating this to be their final moment in life together.

"Ethan, get off me!" Courtenay snapped, shoving him against the footboard of the bed.

Heather turned off the closet light and ushered Courtenay to step inside.

"Good luck." Heather started the stopwatch on her cell phone and took a seat next to Ethan on the bed.

"Don't back out on your promise, Miss Heather."

With an exaggerated exhale, the fourth grader stepped into the darkness and closed the door.

———

COURTENAY EMERGED FROM THE CLOSET FIVE minutes later.

Ethan, hardly able to contain his enthusiasm, leaped from the bed and wrapped his arms around his sister. "You did it!" he shouted elatedly. "You really did it!"

Heather, more than surprised by Courtenay's fortitude, acknowledged the girl's achievement by holding out her hand for a high five. Courtenay ignored it and beamed a smile so unexpectedly strange, Heather and Ethan both reeled at its intensity.

"Your turn," Courtenay said.

Heather batted her eyes and laughed. "Excuse me?"

"It's your turn. You said you had to do this when you were my age, but you only stayed in the closet for a few minutes."

Heather shook her head, disbelieving. "Come again?"

"If you didn't go for the full five minutes," Courtenay smartly repeated, "you couldn't watch the movie. Wasn't that your rule?"

"That didn't apply to me, Courtenay."

"You're still too scared to do it."

"No, I'm not."

"Yes, you are."

"I wouldn't watch the movie if I couldn't handle being scared."

"Then it won't be a problem."

"That's enough, Courtenay. I said the closet doesn't scare me."

"So prove it. I *dare* you."

Heather, with an unwanted strain gnawing at her temples, scratched her head and took a deep breath. She stepped forward and placed her hands on her hips. "Maybe you should just go to bed."

"Then I'll tell my parents you locked me in the closet," Courtenay stated. "I'm sure they would love that."

Heather couldn't believe her ears. Courtenay had never spoken to her like this before. She presumed Courtenay would be excited to watch the movie and was surprised that the girl's focus remained strictly on the closet. Was Courtenay upset about the dare and wanted to get even? Or was she actually scared to watch the movie and deflecting?

Ethan timidly backed away and sucked his thumb.

"If I do this," Heather imparted, "you guys have to promise you won't give me any grief for the rest of the time I'm your babysitter. That means every night I come over, you must do everything I say as soon as I say it. Agreed?"

Ethan nodded from behind the bed.

"What about you, Courtenay? We got a deal?" Heather held out her hand once more, hoping Courtenay would ignore it the same way she did before. Much to Heather's disappointment, Courtenay extended her own puny arm and shook her babysitter's hand, accepting the offer.

The deal was set.

Courtenay grabbed the clock from the nightstand to track the time while Heather did the same with the stopwatch on her phone. She shoved the device into her pocket and stepped into the closet.

"No funny business," the babysitter warned.

The door sealed shut behind her.

Then there was darkness.

———

The first thing Heather noticed about the walk-in closet was the strange smell. It was sour, stuffy, and suffocating.

Heather sat down in front of the door and leaned against it, staring at the soft, yellow light sneaking in between the cracks and spilling onto the carpet in front of her. It comforted her enough to forget the overwhelming darkness and the sour, suffocating smell.

She listened intently with her ear to the door, trying to decipher what the kids were up to. She couldn't be sure, but it sounded like Courtenay was telling Ethan to hide under the bed. Heather predicted they were planning to scare her when she got out. She guessed that was why Courtenay was so adamant about getting her to go into the closet. She imagined Ethan grabbing her ankle from under the bed and faking a scream for him, and she stifled a laugh.

THUMP.

There was another sound from somewhere in the house,

no farther than the back wall of the closet. Heather's eyes widened, trying to see through the darkness but to no avail.

Heather shifted her weight, trying to get comfortable. She reached down to the back pocket of her blue jeans, feeling blindly as she grabbed a lumpy object from inside it.

Her cell phone. For a brief moment, she forgot she even had it.

Heather checked the time. She had only been in the closet for thirty-four seconds. She sighed.

THUMP.

There was the sound again.

Using the glowing blue light of her phone, Heather sat up and guided the device across the clothes rack, admiring the mother's dresses, shirts, jackets, and sweaters. She became so engrossed in the mother's clothes that she forgot the sound she was investigating and elected to pull out the woman's wedding dress. She held it out in front of her, dancing in place, her mind harking back to the time she did the same thing with her own mother's gown.

Then, on her tip toes, Heather rummaged through the boxes on the top shelf. She found old shoes, a collection of baseball cards, a box of old receipts, and an even larger box full of what appeared to be Christmas presents for the kids: a Nintendo Switch, two LEGO toy sets, a box of fake jewelry (which Heather helped herself to), and a unicorn-shaped Squishmallow. Not a bad start for the kids or parents, considering it was still November.

Heather checked her cell phone again. Two minutes and forty-one seconds.

Over halfway there, Heather told herself. Just keep busy.

Heather returned to the closet door and sat down in front of it. She thought about her best friend, Ashley, who was probably having a better time at the bowling alley without her. She texted a message to her and hit SEND on her phone, but the screen froze and searched for a signal. The closet's impenetrable walls prevented her from getting a single service bar. Even worse, the battery icon on her phone was blinking, something it would always do within minutes of shutting down completely.

Four minutes and twelve seconds.

THUMP!

The sound boomed this time, echoing off the walls.

Louder.

Closer.

Inside the closet.

"What the hell?" Heather jumped up and called for the kids. There was the sound of moving feet on the other side of the closet door.

"Are you still alive?" Courtenay joked, her voice muffled behind the thick wooden barrier.

"What are you guys doing out there?" Heather inquired.

"Just sitting on the bed," Courtenay replied. "Thirty seconds left! You're almost done!"

"Ethan's out there, too?"

"Yeah, he's here with me. What's going on?"

"Do you guys hear anything funny?" Heather asked. "Like strange bumping sounds?"

"Nothing funny out here," Courtenay remarked. "Sixteen seconds!"

THUMP!

The sound was even closer this time, almost as if something had fallen out of the clothes rack at the end of the closet.

Heather stood up, unblinking, her cell phone trembling out of her hand.

"Courtenay, did—did you hear that sound?!" she managed to get out, her voice cracking.

"I don't hear anything," Courtenay said, her shadow vanishing from the crack of the door.

THUMP!

Heather bent down, picking up her phone. She checked the time. Just five more seconds, but Heather found herself too scared to move.

THUMP!

Something was *definitely* in the closet with her, slowly moving closer. With all her willpower, Heather turned the cell phone over and pointed the light at the back of the closet.

She screamed.

Dragging itself across the carpet was a small human figure. Its skinned body of exposed muscles and tendons smeared hot blood across the carpet as it closed in on Heather. It reached out to her with a shaking, cadaverous hand that dripped with gore.

Heather shrieked again, falling back against the door. Her heart pounded mercilessly in her chest. Her eyes bulged like two swelling balloons ready to pop.

"What *ARE* you?!" Heather cried, and before the thing in front of her could respond, a piercing scream echoed from the other side of the door. It was Ethan.

Heather turned and pulled at the knob, but the door wouldn't budge. The kids had somehow locked her in as a joke, and now they were in trouble.

"COURTENAY! ETHAN!" Heather screamed, pounding on the door. "RUN! GET OUT OF THE HOUSE!"

Heather looked back, watching the thing in the closet dig its chipped fingernails into the carpet and creep forward. The light of the cell phone reflected off its scalped head—a dome of white bone slicked with a thin layer of pinkish blood.

"Please don't hurt me!" Heather cried, dropping to her knees.

The thing on the floor slowly lifted its head, exposing its skinned face.

Heather froze in disbelief, gawking at the familiar blue eyes staring back at her from the darkness. The thing on the floor lifted its arm once again, revealing a clump of beautiful blonde hair wrapped gingerly in its bloody hand.

"*Miss Heather...*" the thing said weakly.

Heather's jaw dropped as she recognized the voice, and the blue eyes, and the beautiful blonde hair, all coming together in one perfect visual of a precarious fourth grader. Heather's eyebrows slanted, and her entire face drooped downward with the sudden realization.

The thing that walked out of this closet was *not* Courtenay.

"Oh my god..." Heather despairingly watched the skinned girl encase the hair in her fingers and, with an embellished exhale, succumb to eternal darkness.

"No...nooooo..." Heather cried.

For a fathomless amount of time, Heather sat wallowing with fear and remorse, her eyes spilling salty tears down her ghost-white cheeks.

She didn't move. She *couldn't* move.

It was only the familiar voice that stirred her from her trance.

"You were right all along," the thing outside the closet said, a perfect mimic of the fourth grader Heather once knew. The soft yellow light of the doorframe was suddenly impeded by the shadow of a dark figure. "You were right to be afraid of the closet."

Heather didn't respond. Her vocal cords constricted in her throat.

"Not just the closet," came a tiny voice next, a perfect duplicate of little Ethan. "The attic. The basement. *Under the bed.*"

"We're everywhere that's ever scared you," the thing that wasn't Courtenay revealed.

Heather lifted her phone. The battery had died. The screen dimmed to black. And in the suffocating darkness, she could hear something else in the closet moving closer, slowly coming for *her*.

"It will only hurt for a moment," the things outside said.

A pair of sharp talons seized her shoulders, and Heather remembered why she'd never stayed in the closet for the full five minutes all those years ago.

Afterword

I suppose the most common question a writer is asked is, "Where do you get your ideas?"

I must not be a writer because no one's asked me.

Regardless, I'd like to share a few words about each of the stories you've just read.

"The Bad Things We Did" stemmed from my fascination with misunderstandings. I grew up reading the *Amelia Bedelia* books and watching *Rugrats* on Nickelodeon, and it always intrigued me whenever the meaning of something was naïvely misconstrued. The literal interpretations of common phrases were usually played for laughs, and while these moments were certainly amusing, I also found them strangely unnerving. If a misunderstanding was corrected or properly explained in a timely manner, it was funny. If it wasn't, *well…*

The line between comedy and horror is as small as a grain of sand, and that same line can be found in our own life stories —which is why we shouldn't judge each other too harshly. We all do bad things in our lives, whether we intend to or not, and it's often luck that keeps us from doing worse. Danish writer

Villy Sørensen explored some of these ideas in his 1953 short story, "Child's Play," the tale of three boys playing doctor that goes terribly wrong. That story affected me so deeply in my teen years, I'm still haunted by it well into my thirties. Ramsey Campbell further cemented my fascination with the horrors of "playtime gone wrong" with his 1977 chiller, "In the Bag," the story of two kids pretending to be astronauts and improvising a space helmet using a plastic bag. You can imagine how that one ends. In many ways, "The Bad Things We Did" is my love letter to Sørensen and Campbell, who both did it first and undoubtedly better.

"Mind the Gap" was inspired by the true story of Dr. Margaret McCollum, a widow in London who would visit a particular train station every day to hear her late husband's recorded voice give the safety announcement. "Mind the gap," he would say as the train would pull into the station and open its doors. One day, the recording was replaced by an automated voice, and Margaret was (very reasonably) devastated. Hearing of her heartbreak, the people at the train station found her husband's recording, reinstated it for their safety announcement, and even made a CD of the recording for Margaret to keep. It's a beautiful story, one that I think perfectly restores one's faith in humanity. Naturally, as a lover of all things dark and twisted, I couldn't wait to destroy that faith by injecting as much terror into my interpretation as possible.

"The Parachute" was written for an open submission anthology. The brief was to write a coming-of-age horror story inspired by a film from the '80s or '90s. I decided to pay homage to 1994's *The Pagemaster*, a largely unseen film where a kid (played by *Home Alone*'s Macaulay Culkin) seeks shelter from a storm inside a library and comes face to face with a colorful monster. I'd had the idea to write about a play parachute for a while, and this seemed like the perfect opportunity to explore it. Originally, I wanted to write a supernatural tale with an emphasis on body swapping—the kids would go under the parachute and emerge from the other side as someone else—but because I had already explored something similar in "The Thing That Wasn't," I decided to bring in an actual monster instead. Growing up, I loved "The Raft" by Stephen King, and I thought it would be fun to pay tribute to that story in a way that was respectful to the material while still feeling like its own thing. "The Parachute" is my thank you to King for inspiring and entertaining me for so many years.

"The Candy Cane Man" was originally going to be a middle-grade book. It was conceived as the story of two young brothers struggling to get along over their holiday break. I thought it would be more interesting if it centered around a toxic gay couple sharing their first Christmas together. With notable exceptions, I've learned that many writers—gay or otherwise—don't explore the dark side of LGBTQ+ characters in fear of the reactions they'll receive from readers ("You're portraying the community in a negative light! You're canceled!"). As a member of that community, I can attest that some of the best and worst people I've met in my life have been gay men, and they can be as perfectly genuine—or perfectly wicked—as anyone else. I'm proud of the lore I created with this story, and I hope my readers never look at a candy cane the same way again.

"Monstrous" grew from a particular interest in influence culture and people who stage things. Think of the YouTuber pranking a friend already in on the joke, or the TikToker plucking her nose hairs to make herself cry on camera. I specifically recall a video of a woman petting her dog on a livestream for clout, then violently pushing the animal away when she thought the video had ended. I fear we live in a vapid world devoid of genuine human emotion, and whenever we *do* feel something—especially when it's pulled from a virtual source—we don't even realize we've been manipulated to feel that way. Combine this element of dark influence with the basis of "The Three Billy Goats Gruff," a childhood favorite and a perfect mirror to Reed's Machiavellian potential, and this story is the extreme instance of what I believe many of the world's manipulators probably deserve.

"The Knocker-Up" was an idea that transpired so suddenly, it ended up replacing another story in this collection entirely. I had just learned about knocker-ups from a social media post and found them totally compelling. For those who aren't familiar, knocker-ups were real people from the Industrial Revolution who woke others up so they could get to work at the factory on time. This was before alarm clocks were affordable or reliable. Knocker-ups often carried long sticks to tap on high bedroom windows, and sometimes they used a peashooter if the window was out of reach. If the sleeping resident didn't go to the window to make it known they were awake, the knocker-up would go inside the house to make sure everything was okay. I'm sure this sounded well and fine to the average individual, but for me, this was weirdly unsettling and the perfect foundation for a horror story.

"Mercy at the End of Her Life" was inspired by my family's horrible experience living in a neighborhood with a homeowner's association. We had the hardest time trying to make improvements to our home because, whenever we tried to fix or update something, it was met with resistance by those in "power." The HOA's opposition always felt unreasonable, like something out of *The Stepford Wives* ("Your siding can't be that color because everything needs to look the same; you can't build that fence because it will look 'too new' compared to the rest in the neighborhood"). It was the pettiest of nightmares. I always wondered what life must be like for the spouse of a power-hungry HOA president. This story is the result of that wondering.

I wrote "The Thing That Wasn't" in the early part of 2009. I was nineteen. I decided to include it in this collection with relatively few changes to retain as much of its authenticity as possible (and before you even ask, yes, I *did* update the toys Heather finds in the closet). Looking at the story now, it almost feels like an artifact from another time in my life—a time when I was still figuring out who I was and what I was doing, both as a writer and an adult who hadn't even come to terms with his own sexuality yet. Totally unintentional when I wrote it, but upon reflection, I can see this story being written in response to my own fears of never leaving the closet. I'm grateful that wasn't the case.

The story for "The Thing That Wasn't" stemmed from a real-life experience. When I was about five years old, my sister and I begged our parents to let us watch *Pet Sematary* with them (I know, a five-year-old has absolutely no business watching something like that, but hey, this was the nineties). Still, we told our parents we'd do anything to prove we were brave enough to handle being scared. Our parents came up with the idea of us individually going into their closet for five minutes with the lights out as a means of testing our resilience. If we succeeded, we could watch the movie. My sister, who was four years older, completed the task without issue, even going as far as to smirk at me as she victoriously emerged from the closet five minutes later. I tiptoed into the closet behind her and promptly walked right back out. I convinced myself if staying in the closet was such a big deal, then surely there was *something* in there waiting for me—something that my parents knew about and had protected me from until this very moment. I had no intention of discovering what it was, so I said goodnight and went to bed.

The possibilities of what awaited me in the darkness

haunted my thoughts for years, and when I started writing scary stories later in life, that event was one of the first to come to mind and be put to paper.

"The Thing That Wasn't" opened many doors for me. After countless rejections, it was one of the first of my stories to ever be accepted for publication. Thank you, Dennis Smithers, Jr. When I adapted the story to a short screenplay, it was one of the first to ever be picked up by a filmmaker and produced. Thank you, Sara Santini. The story even connected me with amazing horror creators who had somehow discovered it on a whim and had kind things to say—notably, the immensely talented Ryan Spindell, who would later go on to write and direct the fabulous anthology, *The Mortuary Collection*, starring Jacob Elordi and Clancy Brown. Thank you, Ryan.

Because of the success with "The Thing That Wasn't," I started writing more short screenplays. As of this writing, seven short films have been adapted from my work. These short films include *The Doll* (directed by Adam Gambrel, who I now consider a good friend); *The Seamstress* (directed by Tyler Mann and later picked up by Bloody Disgusting as part of their *Bloody Bites* series); and *Hiccups* (directed by Karson Holbrook, which would go on to place in the Top 10 at Shriekfest Film Festival under the short screenplay category). All of this gave me the confidence to continue writing—in any capacity—and never give up my dream of telling stories. It is unlikely any of the other stories in this collection would exist without "The Thing That Wasn't," so I'd be negligent not to include it here. I don't know if the story holds up (it's been fifteen years, after all), but I hope it remains as impactful to readers as it has been for me.

If you'd like to follow my writing journey, you can find me online: @chrishasastory. If you enjoyed this book, please consider leaving a rating and review on Amazon, Goodreads,

Bookstagram, Booktok, the "Books of Horror" Facebook group, or anywhere else that tickles your fancy. Ratings and reviews are a priceless tool for independent authors such as myself, and amazing readers who go that extra mile allow me to continue doing what I love.

Thank you for reading!

Acknowledgments

Many people made this book possible, and I'd be remiss not to recognize their contributions.

Before and above anyone, thank you to my parents, Tina and Jim Shamburger, for your unconditional love and support. Life is a relentlessly changing thing, and through all of it, you have been my constants. Whenever I doubt myself, you encourage me. Whenever I struggle to look on the bright side, you sit with me in the dark. And four years ago, when I hit rock bottom and felt like I'd lost myself, you found me in the empty void and saved me from it. I am so lucky to call you Mom and Dad.

Thank you to my sister, Heather Shamburger, for being the most loyal curator of the many stories I've wanted to tell. There is no doubt in my mind you've been my biggest fan after all these years. Do you remember when we used to play school together, and you made me play the role of the student even though I wanted to be the teacher? I remember.

My deepest gratitude to the actual teachers who nurtured my proficiency in writing as much as my passion for it: Mavis Niino, Stacy Bagwell, Tara Sisino Land, and Kim Baker. I hated school, but I remember all of you with a rare fondness.

Thank you to Caitlin Schonleber Hancock and Courtenay Hicks, two of the strongest women I know, and two amazing souls I have the privilege to call lifelong friends. I am forever grateful to have you both in my life.

A sincere thank you to friends and early readers for their helpful advice and feedback, especially to Marc Schoenbach,

Marissa Segovia, Mark Allan Gunnells, Michael Ballif, Robbie Myles, Thomas Napier, Troy Escamilla, and Jay Bower.

Thank you to SimplyScripts.com, HorrorDNA.com (specifically Steve Pattee), and the "Books of Horror" Facebook group. These online communities undoubtedly strengthened my abilities as a writer and connected me with horror fans from all over the world.

I'd like to thank Kristina Osborn of Truborn Design for creating one of the most gorgeous covers I've ever seen. Without her work to inspire me, "The Bad Things We Did" might have never been written.

Thank you to my editor and friend, Bret Laurie, for your understanding, sense of humor, studious attention to detail, and constant support.

Thank you to my first cat, OJ, who always kept me company during my writing sessions, and who never once stepped foot on the keyboard while I was working. You were the best companion a guy could have. I miss you so much.

Absolutely no thanks whatsoever to my other cats—Binx, Oliver, Chandler, and Joey—who I had to fight tooth and nail to keep off my keyboard while writing this book. If you see a typo, there's a good chance one of them is responsible438qjknz.

Thank you to the following creative geniuses for your influence and inspiration: R.L. Stine, Kevin Williamson, Stephen King, Edgar Allan Poe, Alfred Hitchcock, Eric LaRocca, John Saul, Villy Sørensen, Ramsey Campbell, Adam Cesare, Mike Bockoven, Stephen Graham Jones, and—perhaps more than anyone—Richard Matheson, who could write a short story like no one else.

Thank you to my amazing readers, from the loyal ones who've followed my writing from the very beginning to those just discovering it for the first time.

Finally, and certainly not least of all, my deepest and most heartfelt thank you to my beautiful husband, Kris Archeske, for always being my first reader, my closest listening ear, and my best friend. You're probably throwing a temper tantrum for putting you last, so I'll just remind you that you're first in my eyes and forever in my heart. I love you. Zztt.

About the Author

Chris Archeske has lived all across the United States and beyond, from Southern towns in Alabama and Georgia to more far off localities including Hawaii and Germany. A lover of all things horror, he grew up reading the Goosebumps series and still has his collection of the original sixty-two books. Aside from R.L. Stine, he enjoys and is inspired by the works of Richard Matheson, Stephen King, Eric LaRocca, Daphne du Maurier, John Saul, and Stephen Graham Jones. Today, you can find him in Iowa with his husband and their four cats.